Love Stories (Sort Of)

Love Stories (Sort Of)

Terry Dalrymple

LAMAR UNIVERSITY press

ISBN: 978-0-9915321-3-1
Library of Congress Control Number: 2015931102

Manufactured in the United States of America

Lamar University Press
Beaumont, Texas

For my family, with unconditional love and with thanks for their unconditional love:

Lorraine
Joshua, Sarah E.D., Caroline, and Sylvia
Phillip and Amanda
Sarah L.D. and Jackson

Fiction from Lamar University Press

Gerald Duff, *Memphis Mojo*
Gretchen Johnson, *The Joy of Deception*
Christopher Linforth, *When You Find Us We Will Be Gone*
Tom Mack and Andrew Geyer, editors, *A Shared Voice*
Harold Raley, *Louisiana Rogue*
Jim Sanderson, *Trashy Behavior*
Jan Seale, *Appearances*
Melvin Sterne, *The Number You Have Reached*
Robert Wexelblatt, *The Artist Wears Rough Clothing*

For more information about these and other books, go to
www.LamarUniversityPress.Org

Acknowledgments

The stories in this volume span twenty-five years of writing. While many, many friends and colleagues have, over those years, provided critiques, encouragement, and support, I wish in particular to thank writers Jerry Craven, Drew Geyer, Carol Reposa, Clay Reynolds, Jim Sanderson, Jan Seale, and Gordon Weaver; Angelo State University friends and colleagues Perry Gragg, Mary Ellen Hartje, Jim Moore, Chris Ellery, Troy Reeves, and Laurence Musgrove (the last three of whom are also writers); personal friends Karl and Sherry Wehner and Gardener and Carolyn Wiseheart; and of course my family, to whom this book is dedicated.

All stories in this collection are either new or have been revised—in some cases extensively revised—since their original publications. I am grateful to the editors of the following journals and anthologies for publishing some of the stories in this book.

Amarillo Bay
American Literary Review
Concho River Review
descant
Iron Horse Literary Review
Modern Short Stories
New Growth 2: Contemporary Short Stories by Texas Writers
New Texas
The Redneck Review of Literature, special "DeTEXification" issue
Salvation
A Shared Voice
Texas Five X 5: Twenty-five Stories by Five Texas Writers
The West Texas Sun
Writing Texas

CONTENTS

I. Distance

Distance

You're alone, he says and pauses by her table.

Not anymore, she smiles and sips her vodka and tonic.

The buzz and hum of bar conversation fills the space between them. He takes the chair across from her, leans into the space, feels warmth from the dim candle beneath his chin. Your paper, he says, this afternoon, I enjoyed it very much.

She sips again, ice clinking in her glass. What is it, she asks and smiles wryly, that you enjoyed so very much?

Your voice, he says, and the dress you wore and your wrist when you turned the pages.

An honest man, she says, the first I've met this weekend. She too leans into the space, her elbow on the table, her chin upon her palm.

These people, he says, networking, making careers. They're young, they're eager, they have no time for honesty.

She taps one red fingernail against her glass, looks down into the vodka, then back at him. And you? she says and purses her lips.

Older, he says, with no delusions and no time for lies. He slides his hand across the table, through the distance, and feels the cool dampness of her fingers where they've touched her glass.

Okay, she says and rises.

* * *

You're no one I can love, she says and he says he knows. It's not because of him, she says and fingers her wedding band. I'm trying but it's never because of him.

No problem, he says. He runs his palm over the smooth curve of her hip.

I've married twice before, she says and finds a memory in the space between them that makes her smile.

I've known lust, he says, desire, even affection. Disgust, too, and hatred that manifests as sex. They're enough, I guess, he says and with a fingertip traces her smile.

The hum of humanity twelve floors below is silenced by the hum of the air conditioner and by the plate glass window and by the distance in between.

When I met you in the bar downstairs, he says, I wanted you more than I do right now.

So, she says, why are we here?

Curiosity, he says, or habit. You're not the first.

And she says she knows.

* * *

He smells the coffee first and then her flesh, or the spot where her flesh has lain. I started your coffee, she says, and unhooks the chain on the door.

He blinks to unblur her. I'm wondering, he says, but she says no and closes the door between them.

At the window, he lights a cigarette and feels the cool plate glass against his forehead. Conditioned air stirs his loose tee-shirt, his morning hair, the tobacco smoke snaking toward the ceiling. He spots her, the red skirt, twelve floors below, tries to gauge the distance between them. Twelve floors, a hundred and twenty feet, perhaps, or a hundred and twenty miles. It's a ways, that's all, and it's the same, and it's always the same. He follows the skirt into the shadows of the parking garage, and he sees, or imagines he sees, the soft sway of her hips. He feels their warmth beneath his hands. He smells the brewed coffee, turns from the window, wonders whether the aroma entices or sickens him.

Not Meanin' To Shoot Myself

Third time's the charm, that's how the saying goes, Jason thought as the girl slid into his passenger seat. A charmer himself, he hadn't much considered the saying before because he'd never needed a third time or even a second. The first time had always been his charm. But he considered it now and desperately hoped that it was true.

A natural-born flirt since grade school, he had always been attractive to women of all ages. Now forty-seven, he had only lately had two swings and two misses due to no fault of his own that he could conceive (though his aversion to contemporary pop music might have contributed to the first of the two). But now, here was this girl, Mandy—no, Mindi, he reminded himself, with two i's (over which she no doubt drew little hearts instead of dots)—sliding into the passenger seat of his Audi A6, jet black, with four doors because he sometimes chauffeured his clients her short black skirt scrunching farther up her thighs, dangerously close to revealing whatever she wore or didn't wear underneath. She flashed him a white-toothed smile and blushed when he complimented her legs.

"Beautiful," he said. "Perfect. Like a model's."

Still blushing, she looked down at her legs, then back at him. "Actually," she said, "I'm going to be an anchor woman."

Doubtful, he thought, but he smiled back at her. "You'll make a beautiful one. I'll watch you every night."

She giggled and patted his shoulder. "You're so sweet."

She'd said that when he offered her a ride, too. "You're so sweet," a sure sign that the third time would, indeed, be the charm.

He had met her at Vinny's Vino Bar. Vinny, whose real name was Wacy Ballinger and who hailed from an east Texas farming family, had

3

bought both the bar and his home through Jason when he moved to McKinney. He had planned to name the establishment Wacy's Watering Hole, but Jason had convinced him that a trendier name would attract both a larger and a better class of clientele. Vinny did, in fact, happen to stock a few fine wines, but otherwise there was nothing particularly vino about the bar. Vinny sold more beer and mixed drinks than wine, and the trendy frozen sweet drinks he concocted sold especially well to his young female client base. That's what Mandy—no, Mindi, damn it, Mindi, Mindi, Mindi!—had been drinking when Jason first spotted her.

That Friday after work—his charm had led him naturally into selling high-end real estate, both residential and commercial—he stopped in for a comfort drink after losing, for the first time in his career, an especially lucrative sale.

Vinny delivered his drink. "Feelin' alright?"

Jason shook his head. "Not feelin' too good myself."

Vinny chuckled. "It's a song, right?"

"Right. But unfortunately, it's also true."

"Maybe this'll help." He set the Crown and Coke on a cardboard coaster. "And there's more where that came from."

From his corner table, Jason scanned the room but spotted no familiar faces. Then he scanned the bar, and there sat the girl, an empty bar stool on either side of her. She pursed her full lips and sucked a straw full of colorful frozen dink into her mouth. She swallowed, then checked her phone. She turned to check the entrance. Obviously frustrated, she checked the phone again, then pursed her lips for another suck at the straw. Jason rose and walked casually to the bar stool on her left. When he set his drink on the bar, the girl glanced over at him.

"I'm sorry," he said. "Is this spot taken?"

She shook her head. "Apparently not."

He sat. "Damn," he said, "as pretty as you are you surely didn't get stood up."

She shrugged, finished a sip through the straw. "Sort of. I mean, not exactly. Just some girl friends." She returned her attention to the straw and sucked up the remains of her drink, the straw gurgling as the glass ran dry.

"Can I buy you another?" Jason asked.

4

She shrugged again. "Why not? Doesn't look like I'm going anywhere."

"What are you drinking?"

"Mango-Watermelon Daiquiri."

"Of course." Jason repressed a shudder. "Those are good, aren't they?"

"Really good," she said. "Especially because you can't taste the alcohol."

"Right. That's what you want in a good drink for sure." He motioned to Vinny, who, seeing that Jason had moved to the bar, smiled slyly and walked their way. "Another Mango-Watermelon Daiquiri for the lovely lady." Here he paused. "I'm sorry." He lay his right palm very gently against the middle of her back. "I don't know your name. I'm Jason."

"Mindi," she said, "with two *i*'s, no *y*."

"I love that name. It's as beautiful as you are."

She giggled and grinned, showing a mouthful of very white teeth. "Thanks."

He patted her lightly, then removed his hand from her back and turned back to Vinny. "Another Mango-Watermelon Daiquiri for Mindi and another Crown and Coke for me."

Mindi scrunched up her face. "Eew."

"I know," Jason said. "You can taste the alcohol. But it's been a rough day. I need something strong."

She shrugged. "Whatev'. Sorry about your day."

"Sounds like you're having a rough one, too."

She sucked on her straw, then said, "Sort of. I mean, the day was okay, but tonight's not looking so good." She checked her phone, looked toward the door. "I mean, they were supposed to meet me here, my friends. We graduated from college together two years ago. But we stay in touch, you know, and we were supposed to meet here for a drink before grabbing some dinner and then going to the Atomic. Do you know that club? It's great. This band, The Crabmasters, they're playing there tonight. I swear, they sound just like Coldplay, probably even better. They're great." Finally she stopped and looked at Jason. "I'm sorry. Sometimes I talk too much."

He smiled reassuringly. "Not at all. You have a lovely voice. I like

5

listening to you."

"Thanks." She flashed him another white smile. "You're nice. You remind me of my grandpa."

In mid-sip of his Crown and Coke, he struggled not to choke. He managed to swallow without incident. "Your grandpa, huh?"

"Yeah. He likes to listen to me, too. And he's really nice, like you."

He switched the subject back to her evening plans. Her car was in the shop, so her mother had dropped her at Vinny's on her way to yoga class, and Mindi was to ride with her friends from there. She lived with her mother while she—Mindi—looked for a job, which, besides working at a donut shop near her mother's apartment part-time, she hadn't yet found. Her mother lived in an apartment because Mindi's father had left when Mindi was seven and Mindi's mother couldn't afford to keep the house. But Mindi's mother was doing quite well these days and had begun thinking about buying a house, which Mindi hoped she'd do because she wanted a dog, a teacup poodle, but the apartment didn't allow it.

"Don't you just love them?" she said. "Tea cup poodles. OMG, they're so freaking cute. I could eat them up."

He said he did. He said they were his favorites. "My ex and I," he said, "we had one. But she, my ex, I mean, left me for a guitar player—I don't remember the name of his band—and she took Fifi with her. I don't miss my ex so much anymore, but, God, I miss that little dog."

"Aww," Mindi said and slid off her bar stool. She wrapped her arms around his neck and squeezed. She kissed his cheek. "I'm so sorry. That's so sad."

"Thanks," he said. "That felt good." And he realized that he meant it. The hug had felt spontaneous, it had felt sincere, it had felt sympathetic. He actually did have an ex, and they actually had owned a dog, a chocolate lab named Rex, and she actually had taken the dog when she left him, not for a guitar player, but for a computer geek on his way to New York for a six-figure position in an up-and-coming communications operation. His ex had been ten years his junior, and despite his frequent philandering—he just couldn't help himself—he did, honestly, adore her, and he did love that chocolate lab. It had all come back as he invented the Fifi story, and Mindi's sympathetic hug had indeed comforted him.

But it had also aroused him and inspired him with confidence that he hadn't lost his touch after all.

She looked at her phone, at the door, then at Jason. "I guess I better go. Do you think he'll call me a cab?" She tilted her head toward Vinny at the other end of the bar.

"No need," he said. "I'm leaving, too. I'll give you a ride."

"You're so sweet. That'd be great."

* * *

And now here she was in his car, saying it again—"You're so sweet"—when he complimented her legs. Third time, he thought, is indeed the charm.

"So, where to?" he asked and tried to stop staring at those lovely, toned, smooth legs.

"Just home, I guess. I'll grab some leftovers and then maybe Mom'll be home and can drop me at Atomic."

He started the Audi and considered his next approach. He couldn't risk taking her home and having Mom show up to ruin the mood. And he couldn't offer to take to the Atomic later because he'd despise the music, not to mention that her friends might be there to distract her. He considered a dinner offer, somewhere quiet and dim. But she didn't really seem like a quiet and dim kind of girl.

"Home it, is," he said. "What's the address?" She told him. He backed out of his spot, and as he shifted into Drive, he said, "Hey, do you mind? My place is on the way. My back's acting up and I need a pill."

"Whatev'," she said cheerily. "It's okay with me."

He maneuvered the roads in such a manner that he hoped she wouldn't notice that his place was not exactly "on the way." She seemed not to. He asked questions about being an anchor woman, and she explained that jobs were, like, really hard to find and that the few she'd found always got filled by someone "with experience." "I mean, really," she huffed, "how hard can it be? I look great on camera—all my professors said so—and I keep up with *ET*, so I always know what the stories are. I could do it easy. I'd be great."

He agreed.

At his house, he unlocked the door and then stepped aside to let her enter first. As she passed through the doorway, he lay his hand against her side as if guiding her. "Can I get you something? A glass of wine, maybe?"

She shrugged. "Sure, I guess. As long as it's not that sour kind, you know. What do they call that?"

He guessed at her meaning. "Dry?"

"That's it, dry. I don't like that kind."

He kept his hand on her side and stepped up next to her other side, guiding her to the kitchen. "I'm sure I'll have something you'll like," he said and silently prayed that he still had that bottle of Chateau d'Yquem a grateful client had given him.

Mindi shrugged the long chain of her tiny purse, just wallet sized, really, off her shoulder and dropped the purse onto the long bar separating the kitchen from the dining room. She climbed into one of the tall bar chairs while he located the wine. "Your kitchen is great," she said and fingered the mesh of a wire basket full of onions and potatoes.

Jason uncorked the wine. "Thanks." He fancied himself a bit of a chef and so enjoyed the spacious kitchen, complete with a six-burner stove, a convection oven, and yards of granite counter top. He set a glass of wine in front of her. "See if that suits you." She sipped and nodded. Jason reached for a remote against the wall to his left, pressed a button, and Traffic's original version of "Feelin'Alright?" flooded the room. To his surprise, Mindi bobbed her head to the music and hummed along. "You know this song?"

She nodded. "When I was little, after my dad left, I spent a lot of time at my grammy and grandpa's. Grandpa played this old timey music all the time." She stopped talking to sing along when the chorus struck up: "Feelin' alright? I'm not meanin' to shoot myself."

"You know," Jason said, "the words are actually—" He stopped himself. No need to embarrass her. Better, he thought, stung by her second comparison of him to her grandpa, to correct that misconception. "You know, I'm not really your grandpa's age. But I heard a lot of this music growing up." Born in 1964 he had, indeed, grown up hearing and loving this music, and he had never acquired a taste for the big-hair bands or the Michael Jackson-Madonna-Cindy Lauper kind of sounds that might be considered closer to the music of his generation.

8

She either hadn't heard him or didn't care, for she made no response. "I'm going to get those pills," he said. "Be right back." He rounded the bar, crossed the dining room, and turned left down a hallway. In the bathroom he rattled a bottle of Advil and ran a little water, just for authenticity's sake. "Whole Lotta Love" cranked up as he walked back, and he thought perhaps he should switch to something softer, more romantic. On the other hand, he owned no contemporary pop music and she likely was not a fan of jazz or big band. At least this was familiar to her and might keep her feeling comfortable.

Back in the kitchen, he stood opposite her at the bar. She still bobbed her head to the music. "More wine?" he asked.

"Just a little. It's good." He poured. "Thanks. Hey, where's that bathroom? I gotta pee." Nothing shy about this girl, he thought. Another good sign. He pointed the way, and once he assumed she was safely ensconced, he headed down the same hallway, intending to click on a dim lamp by his bed and light the five candles on his dresser. But the bathroom door remained wide open, and when he instinctively looked in, there she sat.

"Whoa, sorry," he said and turned away.

She just giggled. "No prob, I'm covered."

He glanced back. Her little black skirt bunched around her waist and her little black panties puddled around her ankles, but the important parts were nevertheless out of sight—barely. "No offense," she said, "but not having a bathroom door is kind of weird."

Distracted by the view, he missed a few beats before registering what she had said. "Oh, no, no, there's a door. It's a pocket door."

Clearly tipsy, she giggled again. "A pocket door. What, do you, like, keep it in your pocket?"

"No. Well, sort of." He reached for the brass latch, popped it up, and pulled the door out a few inches. "It's here, in the pocket of the wall."

"Wow. Like magic. Like a secret panel or something. That's great."

He stifled a laugh because he'd be laughing at her, not with her. "Right. It saves space."

"Okay," she said, "I'm gonna finish up. You gonna keep watching?" Much as he wanted to, he said no and pulled the door to.

With no time now to light the candles while she was occupied, he

9

walked back to the kitchen. She, too, returned and climbed up onto her chair.

"More wine?" Tipsy was good, he thought. Not drunk, just tipsy.

"I shouldn't," she said. "I'm kinda feeling it, you know?"

"Sure," he said. "Okay."

"But maybe just a little." She grinned her bright white grin. He poured. Bob Dylan sang "Blowin' in the Wind," and again she hummed along and again she fingered the wire mesh basket. "The thing is," she said, "about this music, you know, a lot of it doesn't make much sense."

"I guess not," he agreed.

"I mean, like this song. I guess it's about nature and all that stuff, but I don't really get "The ants are my friends, just blowin' in the wind."

"No, it's," he began but once again stopped himself. "I don't really get it either."

She moved her hand from the basket to its contents and began shuffling potatoes and onions as if she were after something. "I mean, I don't know, I guess ants are pretty light. Maybe they can blow in the wind. I've never seen one blow in the wind, but I guess it could happen. Do you think it could happen?"

He laughed and laid his hand against her cheek. "What I think is that you are absolutely precious." He considered for a moment, then added, "You're great."

She smiled. "Hey, look." She fished a potato from the bottom of the basket and held it up in front of him. "That's great," she said.

He studied the misshapen potato. "It's a heart."

"Yeah," she beamed. She turned it over. "Or a butt. Or boobs." She giggled.

"Exactly," he said. "But nowhere near as beautiful as yours."

She straightened in her seat and pushed out her chest. "They are pretty great, aren't they?"

He nodded. "Better than great. They're perfect."

"Hey," she beamed, "wanna see something?" She slipped the top button of her blouse undone and pulled the blouse aside to reveal a significant portion of her right breast and the rim of her black bra. In the soft flesh of the lovely white breast, just outside the bra line, she sported a small, bright red heart tattoo. "Heart and boob, see? Like the potato."

He stared. "Much better than the potato."

"You are the sweetest," she said. "I've got one on my right butt cheek, too."

"I'd love to see it."

"It's just like this one. Right in the big fat middle of my butt cheek." She giggled almost uncontrollably.

He leaned onto the counter, his face just inches from hers. "Listen, why don't we kick off our shoes, put our feet up and get to know each other." He nodded vaguely in the direction of his bedroom.

"We know each other," she giggled. "You're Jason, I'm Mindi— remember, two *i*'s no *y*—and we both like Vinny's and you—" She stopped suddenly and looked in the vague direction he had indicated, then back to his face. "Wait, did you mean—" Her face scrunched and she blurted, "Eew!"

Jason visibly flinched. "Eew?"

"Sorry. No offense. It's just, you know, you're, like, old."

Eew. You're old. At least the previous two hadn't acted disgusted, just politely eased away before, he told himself, he had a chance to work his magic. Had they, too, thought eew?

"I'm sorry, Mindi. I didn't—"

She waved his words away. "No prob. You're not the first old guy to hit on me. But you are definitely the sweetest." She leaned in and kissed his cheek. "Really, you're great. But, you know."

She was truly precious. He'd been a fool, and a lecherous fool at that. "Yes, I know. Listen, you're a lovely girl with a tender heart." He grinned. "The real one, not the boob one."

She smiled back. "Hey, the boob one's pretty great."

"Yes," he said. "It's pretty great." He straightened. "So, I should take you home."

"I'll just grab a cab."

"No," he said.

"Yes," she said.

He relented. "Okay. But at least let me call."

He called, gave his address, said the driver should honk when he arrived. But he needn't have bothered with the last instruction because Mindi had already scooped up her tiny purse and headed toward the front door. He followed.

On the front porch, they stood in awkward silence until she said, "Really, it's okay. You're great."

"Not sure," he said. "But you are definitely great."

She stepped over to him, hugged him tightly, then stepped back. "Maybe we'll see each other. You know, at Vinny's or something."

"Maybe."

The cab arrived, and she was gone.

Back inside, he sat at the kitchen bar, staring down at the granite countertop. Eew. You're old. For the first time in his life, he knew it was true. He was old. Forty-seven. Almost fifty. He'd never heard of the Crabmasters, nor did he care. He knew the words to "Feelin' Alright?" and "Blowin' in the Wind." He owned a house with a pocket door.

Eew. You're old. God, he was twice her age. He'd struck out three times, and to top it off he'd lost his first sale ever. He was old. He'd lost his touch. He was done. He needed to reassess. And he needed a drink. But not here. Not alone. He needed movement. He needed noise. He needed distraction. He grabbed the heart-shaped potato she'd left on the counter and dropped it in the trash. He headed for Vinny's.

* * *

As he expected, business at Vinny's had grown since he'd been there earlier. He parked several rows out. As he approached the entrance, he smelled cigarette smoke, and when he stepped into the light at the door, a cloud of it wafted into to his face. He waved it away and detected a whiff of cloyingly sweet perfume as well.

"Sorry," a woman's voice said. He peered beyond the light where she stood in semi-darkness, the cigarette glowing between her fingers. "It's a bad habit, I know."

Despite his growing depression, the old habits kicked in. "No problem. I used to smoke," he said, although he'd never touched a cigarette in his life. "Still love the smell."

"You're probably lying," the voice said. "But you're sweet to say so."

You're sweet. It's what Mindi had said. "That perfume," he said, "that's what I like smelling."

She stepped into the light, crushed her cigarette out in the ashcan near the door. "Quite the charmer, aren't you?"

She appeared about his age and somehow familiar. Did he know her? Unlikely. He had dated only two women his age and those only briefly. But surely he'd remember if she were one of them. She wore tan slacks and a bright red pullover blouse, moderately vee-necked. Not spectacular, he thought, but not bad. He opened the door and motioned for her to go first.

"You're a gentleman," she said and bowed slightly before entering.

He spotted one empty stool at the bar and approached it. She followed. "Please," he said. "Help yourself." He motioned to the stool.

"Thanks. But I'm just getting a drink."

He sat. Vinny, drawing a beer for another customer, waved that he'd be there shortly. Jason studied the woman. A little thick in the middle, but not fat. Face, perhaps a bit puffy, but smooth and attractive. She had attempted to disguise slight bags under the eyes with make-up. And the eyes, bright, lively, and again somehow vaguely familiar.

"I'll be happy to buy your drink," he said.

"Thanks, but I'm with friends." She pointed a thumb over her shoulder to some table behind them. "My yoga group. We're celebrating a year together."

"Yoga. That's healthy. Congratulations."

Vinny arrived and took her order first. Gin and tonic. Good for her, she liked the taste of alcohol.

Vinny fetched the drink, and when he returned Jason said, "It's on me." The woman turned to him. "I know," he said, "the yoga group. But it's still on me."

She raised her glass. "Cheers."

"And to you."

"The usual?" Vinny asked, and that's when it struck Jason. The familiar look, the familiar eyes, the yoga group. "Wait," he said to the woman's back. She stopped, turned. "Are you by any chance related to someone named Mindi, two *i*'s, no *y*?"

The woman looked surprised. "You know Mindi?"

"We've met. Sweet girl."

"My daughter," she smiled. "Sweet, yes, but I wish she'd find a real

13

job."

"Daughter? I would have guessed sister."

"You are a silver-tongued devil, aren't you?"

"I mean it. You're lovely."

She raised her glass once more. "And you, sir, are bullshit. But you're the best bullshit I've heard in a long time. To your health and happiness." She sipped the gin and tonic.

"Mindi said," he blurted before she could get away, "that you might be looking for a house." He slipped a business card out of his shirt pocket. "If you need anything, give me a call."

She read the card. "Thanks. I just might." She tucked the card down her vee-neck, presumably into her bra, then turned and walked to a table seating four other middle-aged women. Middle-aged, he thought. Not old.

He faced the bar. "Feelin' alright?" Vinny said.

He considered the question, nodded. "Not meanin' to shoot myself."

The Sexual Exploits and Eventual Disappearance of Cole Walker, Brilliant Bio-technologist

Hopelessly romantic as a boy, Cole Walker was nonetheless destined by his family of scientific geniuses to become an accomplished bio-technologist. "I want to write novels," he once told his father, an inventor of twenty-three automated gadgets, seven of them Ronco's top sellers.

"Nonsense," his father replied while studying his intricate drawings of an automated banana slicer.

"I want to hitch-hike around the country and live off the land," he told his mother, a writer of science books for children, three of which had each been adopted by school systems in at least twenty-two states.

"Don't be silly," she said, at the same time tapping a forefinger against her jaw and pondering the chapter title she had just typed into her computer: "Chapter 3: The Quirky Quark."

He said nothing to his older brother, whom he'd have to call in Dallas, where the boy had enrolled in medical school at the age of seventeen.

And so he became a bio-technologist.

He spent his college years in classrooms, libraries, and labs, so immersed in his studies that he neglected the other sorts of passions he had once known. But when he landed a prestigious position in her father's private laboratories in Austin, he met Cheryl, and another passion overwhelmed him by clamoring for release, demanding attention. Specifically, demanding Cheryl.

He pursued her diligently, and she just as diligently rebuffed him. Something troubled her, he felt certain when he looked into her eyes, and those troubled eyes somehow endeared her to him. Well, he had to admit, her perky boobs helped, too. He wanted to hold her, comfort her, dispel her troubles. He wanted, in short, to be her savior and, to be honest, to lay her. For two years he dreamed about doing exactly that.

His dreams came true when her father died.

He stood beside her at the funeral, and she clutched his hand and wept. Afterwards, he took her to his apartment to recuperate and she thanked him with open legs. He reveled in the unbelievably passionate lovemaking—though in truth, he thought later, his inexperience might have made regularly passionate lovemaking or even dispassionate lovemaking seem unbelievably passionate. In any case, she rocked his world once, twice, and then flew off to Aruba.

He assumed that she went to straighten out the affairs of her father's vacation home, and he vowed to wait for her no matter how long her business took. He redirected his newly blossoming passion back into his work and established a reputation as one of the top researchers in the company. And then an old friend of her father's told him that Cheryl had moved to Malaysia.

Cole winced. "Malaysia? Why?"

The portly man shrugged and handed him a postcard from Malaysia. The message read, "No more vacation home." She had not signed the card, but Cole recognized her small, tightly-formed hand-writing.

For five days straight, Cole called in sick and spent every hour combing the internet for mention of her or clues to her exact whereabouts. He found nothing, not a single lead, not a single word. She had simply disappeared into Malaysia, it seemed, settling anonymously somewhere among its twenty million or so residents. Maybe, he thought, she was hitch-hiking around that country and living off the land. Lucky her.

And he vowed to wait for her. He felt certain she would someday return and be so moved by his chaste faithfulness that she would fall—no, swoon, he amended—into his arms and ask him—no, beg him—to make mad passionate love with her, now and for the rest of their lives.

In the meantime, he continued building his reputation in the bio-technology community. He earned a large salary and managed to save ample portions of it because he lived a quiet life. He cooked his own meals which, though it wasn't living off the land, did at least make him feel self-sufficient. And because he lived chastely, he rarely went out except for an occasional beer with one of his team members or a glass of wine with his administrative assistant, Georgia, who claimed to be a lesbian and thus posed no threat to his sexual restraint. Georgia admitted that she loved the company of men, but the thought of one touching her body with his repulsed her. On the other hand, she said, she sometimes thought she'd like a woman's body touching hers, but she found women vapid and, thus, hated keeping company with them.

Once, in a small bar near his apartment complex, they watched a significantly drunk middle-aged woman rub herself against a widely grinning man perched on a bar stool. Cole, who had downed one chardonnay too many, thought of Cheryl. He said, "There's a lucky guy," to no one in particular. But since Georgia sat across from him, the comment seemed directed at her.

"Yuk!" she said.

"Really, it's not so bad," he said and poured his second glass of wine too many. Georgia's face scrunched in disgust at virtually the same moment Cole suddenly perceived her as quite pretty. He said, "Well, I've only done it twice. But I sure did like it." Not beautiful pretty, he thought, but plainly pretty. Her auburn hair, cut short, looked silky, and it glowed softly in the dim light of the bar.

Georgia shuddered. "I've never done it. Not even with myself."

She had a nice figure, he thought. True, she typically wore a baggy button-up shirt tucked into baggy slacks that downplayed her figure. Still, he felt quite certain it was a shapely enough figure. His long months of abstinence, coupled with his inebriation, coupled, in turn, with his new perception of Georgia, somewhat modified the terms of his vow in his foggy brain. She was simply a friend, and a lesbian friend at that. Sex with her wouldn't even really count as a transgression, would it?

"Well," he said, then paused. He averted his eyes from hers and looked at his wine glass instead. "We're just friends and, you know, if you, just as friends, you know, ever wanted to try it, you know, to see if, well, you know, you might like it."

Perhaps because she, too, had imbibed some drinks too many, she didn't, as he had expected, shove back her chair and run screaming out of the bar. Her elbow on the table, her cheek in her palm, she stared across the table, expressionless. "Hmmmm," she finally said.

17

He paid for their drinks, and they stumbled to his apartment. In the bedroom, he reached to unbutton her blouse. She stepped back. "Don't touch me," she snapped. Then, perhaps remembering the point, she softened and added, "I'll do it myself." And she did. She did not seem particularly uncomfortable allowing him to look at her, but when he removed his clothes and stood naked in front of her, a spontaneous "Eeeww" escaped her lips. Her body, as he had guessed back in the bar, was not so bad. Her breasts were small, perhaps hardball sized, but still firm and smoothly rounded. Her torso was a bit elongated, and her hips created no lovely curves, but they were bare and smooth, and he was stirred.

She inhaled deeply, exhaled audibly, then said, "Okay," more to herself than to him. "Okay," she repeated and climbed onto the bed. She lay on her back, hands tightly at her side, legs pressed together. When he eased onto the bed beside her, her muscles visibly tightened, and when he reached to touch her she recoiled and pushed his hand away. She took another deep breath and tried to relax her board-stiff muscles. "Okay," she whispered, her voice trembling. "Try again."

This time, his palm actually made contact with her breast, but as soon as it did, her hand slapped it away. She made a noise in her throat that he thought might have meant "Sorry," but it might just as well have meant "Yuk." His stirrings progressively diminishing, he suggested they skip that part and get straight to the main event. She nodded but looked terrified. He straddled her, careful that no part of him touched her, his legs and arms several inches from her flesh on either side of her. He looked down at his presumed target. "Listen," he said gently, sympathetically, "I'm sorry, but you'll have to spread your legs for this to work." She tried, failed, then tried again and managed to make a little space for him there. He eased into position without contacting her. She closed her eyes, inhaled deeply, and held her breath. But when his flesh touched hers, she flinched, and her right leg jerked up and smacked his most tender body parts. He grunted. She gagged, rolled quickly, and wretched over the bedside. The violence of her movement dumped him into a naked heap on the floor just inches from whatever her stomach had emptied.

Tailbone throbbing, he arose and dressed and then mopped up the floor with a towel while she dressed. They never went out for drinks together again.

He missed his nights out with Georgia but comforted himself with the fact that his vow of chastity until Cheryl returned had not been tainted. Nights when he might have otherwise sipped wine with Georgia, he sat on his small balcony overlooking Town Lake and daydreamed about Cheryl's return. And there, on that balcony, is where he first began mentally sketching his novel. It would be a thriller, a novel of international intrigue centered, of course, on bio-technology. There would be much spying, much double-crossing, many experiments secretly sabotaged. There would be many nerve-wracking chases on foot, by car, by boat, maybe even by plane. There would be gun fire and explosions. And there would be sex. Lots and lots of sex. He and Cheryl would be the central characters, though of course he'd change their names, and most of the sex would be theirs.

When those scenes appeared in his head, he became too agitated to think clearly and so would turn to the sale of the novel instead. The advance and the royalties, along with all the money he was saving, would be plenty. When Cheryl returned, he would take her away somewhere wonderful. Maybe they'd hitch-hike around the country for a time and then settle down on a small piece of land. They'd grow their own vegetables, fish for their food, maybe hunt, too, though he had never even touched a rifle. They would swim naked in a stream and make love on its soft, grassy banks. But there was the sex again, and the agitation. And so he would go to bed and force himself to ponder some bio-technological breakthrough he might be on the brink of.

Although even small breakthroughs occurred infrequently, he became more and more renowned for his brilliant work. His parents were proud, he felt certain, despite the fact that, busy as they were with their own work, they never called and never answered if he called. And his brother was far too busy being a famous surgeon who also provided medical commentaries for CNN and consulted with writers and directors of three different medical dramas.

Cole traveled frequently, attending conferences and visiting cutting-edge bio-tech laboratories around the world. Exactly seventeen months after the Georgia debacle, he sat in a conference room in Hong Kong in a session titled "Reinstallation of the Dead via Bio-computechnology: Possibilities and Projections." A graying, pudgy scientist ten or fifteen years his senior sat in the chair to his left. Her nametag identi-fied her as Dr. Gayla Bastrop from a government agency in London. Dr. Gayla Bastrop embraced the session's topic enthusiastically. Occasionally, she turned to Cole and whispered, lips ever-so close to his ear, "Isn't it fascinating?" or "How amazing!" At one high point in the presentation, she clutched his leg, not far from the area once crushed by Georgia's flailing leg, and whispered heatedly, "I'm positively aflame with excitement!" Her soft, lilting voice and lovely British accent, her breath against his ear, and her hand on his thigh created sensations he had struggled to suppress and avoid.

His concentration completely derailed, he spontaneously squeezed her meaty thigh and whispered, "Me too!"

Afterwards, she invited him to her room for a glass of Gold Label Dynasty Merlot. During the first glass, they—she, in particular—babbled excitedly about the possibilities of bio-compu-techno reinstallation and scooted closer and closer to him on the couch with every comment. She complained of heat and unbuttoned the top two buttons of her white cotton blouse. She rose and fetched the Dynasty to pour a second round, and, after pouring his, leaned in close and said, "Dr. Cole Walker, you positively jiggle my jelly." She leaned farther into him and buried his mouth and nose in her ample cleavage. He inhaled the flower-sweet perfume she had dabbed between those pillowy-soft mounds and com-pletely forgot the little remnant of his vow he'd been desperately clinging to. Her jelly did, indeed, jiggle, all voluptuous and soft and warm against his flesh, and their first encounter concluded quickly, which she said was perfectly fine because it left more time for additional encounters. And she was right, for by morning they had added two more. Later, when he awoke, he felt fully reinstalled.

Guilt niggled him a bit, but he dismissed it with the thought that it was only one small transgression in almost two years. Or, technically, did he have to count it as three? No matter, it was just one woman—Georgia definitely didn't count—just a brief respite from his vigilance.

And so he renewed his vow to stay pure until Cheryl returned.

He bought a small gas grill for his balcony and cooked on it at least three nights a week. It still wasn't living off the land, but it seemed some-how more rustic, more elemental than indoor cooking. He also began walking anywhere he needed to go within three miles of his apartment. It wasn't hitch-hiking, but as vehicles raced by he could imagine shoving his thumb in the air, clambering into a stranger's car, striking up a conversation, and rolling miles away from a job at which he continued to excel but which inspired him less and less every day.

Twenty-three months after he enjoyed the jiggling of Dr. Gayla Bastrop's jelly, he committed another small transgression with a skinny waitress in D.C. Newly arrived, he stopped in the hotel restaurant for a burger. Shortly, the waitress greeted him pleasantly with a big smile and a gentle pat on the shoulder. Her name tag said "Gracie." When she brought his burger, to which she had added a generous helping of fries at no charge, she patted his shoulder again and asked, "Do you want anything else?" Had she winked at him when she asked that question? No, he thought, surely not. He had misperceived. As she maneuvered through the room, taking orders, delivering food, clearing dishes, she stopped frequently by his table, patted or squeezed his shoulder, asked if he wanted something else, and, when business slowed, made small talk. Why was he in D.C? Was it his first time? Where was he from? Was he staying in the hotel? Was his wife with him? Her attentions and touches reminded him that he did, indeed, want something else. Mostly, he wanted Cheryl. But Cheryl wasn't here. And Gracie was.

He watched Gracie's movements, her short gold skirt slapping pertly against her long skinny legs with every step. Granted, she was homely, with stringy brown hair and a pock-marked face and the body of a thirteen-year-old despite the fact that she would never see thirty again. But she had a lovely smile and a soft touch, and the more he watched her skirt slap against her legs the sexier those skinny—no, he amended, slender—legs appeared to him. She brought his ticket and asked if he was sure he didn't want anything else. He hesitated, and she added, "I mean, I'm off in fifteen. I could show you around the city or something."

He stared at her name tag, and suddenly it hit him: Gracie. Why of course, Georgia, Gayla, and now Gracie. It was a sign. All women whose names started with G, the same letter that began the words *grant* and *grace* and *good* and *go ahead*. And Gracie, a woman named for grace, stood there offering to grant him grace; it would be good; he should go ahead.

She provided a knowledgeable tour around the city, and afterwards walked him to his room and offered an even more knowledgeable tour of her body, which, despite its appearance of bony hardness, proved elastic and pliable and incredibly inventive in ways he had never imagined. There was certainly none of Georgia's stiff-armed, clench-legged terror here, but, rather, spread-eagle legs and long extended arms inviting him into an embrace which, of course, he accepted enthusiastically. There was certainly none of Dr. Gayla Bastrop's jiggling jelly here, no soft voluptuous flesh, but neither was there any of Dr. Gayla Bastrop's limited ability to bend and stretch nor preference for traditional positioning. Where and how did she learn these things, he wondered, but he didn't really want to know. He'd renew his vow tomorrow, he knew. But for now, he was the lucky recipient of Gracie's generous helpings, and for now was all that mattered.

When he woke, the bed was otherwise empty. She had left a note written on hotel stationary in large, loopy handwriting: "Off to work. If you're ever in D.C again . . . Love and kisses (oh, and that other thing, tee-hee), Gracie."

Oh, yes, he thought and smiled, that other thing. Did he have to count it in his transgressions? Four last night if he counted it, just three if he didn't. No, he assured himself, it didn't really count. But he sure hoped Cheryl would learn it when she returned to him.

Back at home, Cole felt fully refreshed but not as willing to immerse himself in work. He still worked, of course, but with less intensity and fewer successes. He bought a small tent and drove over to McKinney Falls State Park. He was awkward setting up the tent but felt sure he would get better with time. He built a small charcoal fire in the designated grill and cooked two hot dogs. They tasted especially good. He slept very well, arose early, and walked to the falls. He sat listening to the music of the water and daydreaming about Cheryl's return. He would bring her camping. He hoped she liked it here. He bet that Gracie certainly would, adventurous a spirit as she seemed to be. Then he chastised himself for thinking of anyone but Cheryl, and began thinking through more of his novel.

Another time, he studied a map to find other parks. He found Bastrop State Park, just east of Austin. He chuckled to himself, thinking of Dr. Gayla Bastrop. If he went to that park, he'd be entering Bastrop again. He considered the pun quite clever. But then he shook his head and tried to think of Cheryl.

Eventually, he camped in Bastrop. He cooked over charcoal, took long walks in the woods, and pondered his novel. He drove through the town, where he discovered The Grace Miller restaurant, called Gracie's by the locals. He began making frequent trips to the park, always eating at least one meal at Gracie's.

One Monday after just such a trip, he said good morning to Georgia, who had remained his faithful administrative assistant all these years. Their relationship was friendly but had never been personal since that disastrous attempt they had made. He felt bad about that disaster, which, he had come to realize, was as much due to his ineptitude as to her inability. She had, at least, been willing, had seemed sincerely curious. Perhaps had he been more experienced he might have suggested something that would have eased her through it. Often, he had wanted to apologize, but he did not wish to embarrass her.

That Monday morning when he greeted her, he walked on to his office before registering that—and he felt quite sure of this—she'd been wearing lipstick and, perhaps, a little eyeliner. And, come to think of it, her blouse fit more snugly and looked more feminine—muslin, he thought, pleated in the front. He did not sit down, instead immediately circling back to her desk. He had been right. She'd grown her hair out, something he should have noticed before, and it fell just to her shoulders in silky waves. Her lipstick was a very pale pink, and the muslin blouse with pleats looked quite lovely on her.

He stood and stared, and she smiled sweetly up at him. "Yes," she said. "It's me." She pushed her wheeled chair back and gestured toward her lap with open palms. "See. Even a skirt." The black skirt most likely fell to just above her knees, but the hem had ridden up and revealed several inches of upper leg. Her legs were slender and shapely. Seeing them, Cole recalled those few moments when she stood naked before climbing into bed. He remembered the stirrings he had felt. And he began to feel them again.

"It's a man," she said. "A very beautiful man in my apartment complex." She looked so much more feminine than before, and even, he thought, a little coquettish the way she dipped her head slightly, looked up at him from partially lowered lids, the hint of a smile playing on her pink lips. "He asked me out." Stirred as he had become, Cole perhaps looked disappointed, for she quickly added, "But I didn't go."

He collected himself. "Maybe you should."

"Oh, I want to. But well, you know." He nodded. She laid her palm along the hem of her dress, her fingers draped over her leg, their tips brushing her inner thigh. She averted her eyes. "I've been practicing. You know, by myself." Though he tried diligently not to do so, Cole nonetheless scanned a mental image of her practicing. He grew warm.

"Well," he said as if bringing the conversation to a close.

Before he could step away, she blurted, "Would you?"

"What?"

"Would you, you know, just as friend, you know, help me try again?"

Of course, he thought, and wanted to help her right there and then, right on top of her desk. His throat constricted and he could not answer.

"It's important," Georgia said and seemed almost pleading. "I want to, you know, with him. But not until I know for sure that I can."

Her apartment was closer, but the beautiful man might see them, so she insisted on Cole's. In his bedroom and in a hurry, he began unbuttoning his shirt. She raised a palm as if to stop him. "One other thing," she said, "I figured out. I think I can do it if I'm in charge, you know?"

He didn't know, but he didn't care. He agreed. And then he found out what she meant. And he liked it very, very much.

Afterwards, they lay exhausted and she talked of the beautiful man and he told her about Dr. Gayla Bastrop. "I must learn that," she said. "I must try that traditional positioning." And they did. And she liked it very, very much. And then he told her about Gracie, and she wanted to learn what Gracie knew. And so throughout the afternoon and long into the night, she practiced and practiced. She wasn't, he knew, as accomplished as Gracie, but, now in full swing, she was certainly as enthusiastic, and he liked it very, very much.

In the early morning, when they knew they should sleep, he couldn't resist telling her about that other thing. Of course, she wanted to try it. She did very well, and then she suggested that he try it. And he did. He thought it was good and she said it was good, and so it was good.

In the morning, she thanked him profusely and said now she couldn't wait to go out with the beautiful man. He wished her well and thought he couldn't wait for Cheryl's return. True, he had added one—or was it six?—more transgression against his vow of abstention until she returned. But he clung to her memory still and, thus, vowed yet again to remain chaste until her return.

Cole continued his camping adventures. He even considered hitch-hiking to Bastrop once, but changed his mind because reports predicted rain. When camping, he wasn't exactly living off the land, but at least he was living on the land and that seemed to him a pretty close second. He considered actually beginning to write his novel but hadn't quite worked out the resolution in his head and decided to do that before sitting down to the computer—no, he reminded himself, pen and paper would be better, more personal, more creative somehow. He plugged along at work but didn't care much about it and even turned down an opportunity to work for a month with a renowned German colleague in Munich.

And finally, seven years, one month, two days, and three-and-a-half hours after leaving for Aruba, Cheryl returned to Austin. Cole was ecstatic and told her all about his seven-year vigil, leaving out the transgressions, at least for now. She called him sweet. He wished, of course, to make love with her immediately, but in deference to her mission he did not ask. Having more or less run away from her father's death, she had returned, she said, to come to terms with it. He said he would help if he could. He stood by her in everything she felt she needed to do, and when, after three days, she declared herself reconciled, he took her to his apartment to recuperate from the emotionally exhausting experience. She appreciated his help and thanked him with open legs.

And he was massively disappointed.

She allowed him his way, sure enough, but she offered nothing but her body parts to the transaction. Afterwards, she rolled away from him and snored. When she awoke, he asked her what she had done in Malaysia. She propped herself against two fat pillows and said , "Nothing much.

Just hung out." He asked her about Malaysian culture. She shrugged. He asked her about the Malaysian countryside. She said she'd never seen it. He asked her about Malaysian government. She said she didn't know. "I guess," she said, "I didn't pay much attention." Georgia, he thought, would call her vapid, and he remembered all their conversations over wine. She spoke passionately about politics and sports and cultural trends and her work, not to mention, though he couldn't help mentally mentioning it to himself, her impassioned attempts to discover her heterosexual abilities and, most importantly, her dynamic success at doing so. He remembered Gracie's thorough knowledge of the history and culture of the city in which she lived and her even more thorough knowledge of what her body could do to please the both of them. He remembered Dr. Gayla Bastrop's impassioned response to scientific possibility as well as her impassioned response to his body and the jiggling of her jelly. He remembered, too, his realization that, because of his virginal state, he might have confused unbelievably passionate lovemaking with regularly passionate lovemaking or even dispassionate lovemaking seven years earlier.

"Cheryl," he said, "what we did just now, did you enjoy it?"

She stretched, then shrugged. "I can take it or leave it."

"And before, seven years ago, did you feel the same way?"

She yawned. "I guess. I really don't remember."

Didn't remember? She didn't remember the most significant moment of his life, the moment, the love, the passion he had held onto for all these years, remaining chaste—well, more or less—as he waited, not even knowing when she might return? "Then," he said, "why bother?"

"Silly," she said, "because you love me, you help me, you take care of me. I appreciate it. I don't mind giving you a treat now and then."

Her words stunned him into silence. So she said, "You seem sad." She untied the sash of her robe and opened the robe fully. "Do you need another treat?"

At no point had she said she wanted him or loved him, nor had she said that he, too, was a treat for her. Still, looking at her lovely naked body, he thought it might be enough. After all, he had the woman he'd saved himself for, more or less, all these years. He had her, and he could have her now and then, she had said. Maybe that was enough, he thought. But when he spoke, his words surprised him. "I'll pass," he said.

Cheryl smiled kindly, retied her robe, scooched down to a prone position, and rolled onto her side. "I'm awfully tired."

He watched her until she snored lightly and then he rose and dressed. He left his apartment complex and walked aimlessly for some time. He stopped in an all-night convenience store for a bottle of water, and as he carried it to the counter he passed a small stack of spiral notebooks, wide rule. Two steps past the stack, he paused, then backed up two steps, pondered, and selected one with a blue cover. It reminded him of open skies. He found Bic pens nearby and selected a blue one. As the sleepy-eyed, scruffy-faced young man rang up his purchase, he opened the spiral to its first page and wrote, centered on the top line, "Chapter 1."

Pen in pocket, notebook and water in hand, he headed east. When he reached I-35, he clambered over the guard rail. He set his water bottle on the ground. Bye-o, Cheryl, he thought. Bye-o, technology. He considered the pun quite clever. And, still clutching the notebook in his left hand, he raised his right arm and stuck his thumb in the wind.

Nasty Things

The last time Felicia Winstock saw Daniel Alldon, she spoke of Jesus washing her feet. To understand why, you would probably have to understand how she had ended up in Dr. Melinda Floyd-Hendricks' Speak Up Center in South Carolina, originating, as she did, from Preston Hollow in Dallas, Texas. But that would require knowing about the harelip—staff at the speech therapy center he attended taught participants to refer to his malady as a cleft lip—she met at the Tell It To Me Slowly Center in Dallas. And even that would require knowing about her husband's death—or disappearance—at sea during their honeymoon cruise, a husband she met while attending a variety of group therapy gatherings for dealing not just with speech impairment but with such matters as auditory impairment, visual impairment, alcoholism, drug addiction, parental dementia, spousal abuse, spousal death, pet death, unnatural relationships with pets, and so forth. But you'd have to know why she attended those gatherings, which would lead you back to what the high school quarterback attempted to do to her during her sophomore year in high school. But the trauma the high school quarterback created can only be understood in terms of her upbringing. Let's face it, we should simply begin at her birth.

Felicia Marie Winstock was born beautiful and intelligent and rich and perhaps a month or so earlier than her parents' wedding date might lead one to expect. Her father, William Carl Winstock, was tremendously wealthy, in large part thanks to his grandfather's and father's amassing of fortunes, although he, too, earned a stunning living as a family attorney for the financially elite in Dallas, Texas. Her mother, Ariel Constance Winstock nee Caruthers, was exceedingly lovely and bright but did not work because—well, because she did not have to. She was, however, quite generous with her time and her husband's money, not to mention her own small inherited fortune. She engaged in much volunteer work and most especially enjoyed her role as a patron—or, rather, matron—of the arts in Dallas, Texas.

Felicia grew up beautiful and smart with all of the advantages excessive wealth and elite social connections can provide. Still, she had a tender soul and treated everyone kindly, including those her mother said were beneath her. She did not always understand the things her mother said, one of which, when she was eight, being that boys liked to do nasty things to girls and that she should be ever-vigil about not allowing those things to be done to her. At the time, they were in Neiman's shopping for a pretty dress that Felicia would wear to Brenda Joy Stillwater's birthday party. Boys would be in attendance as well.

"What things, Mother?" she wanted to know.

Ariel scrunched her face and shuddered. "Never mind," she said. She held a pale blue dress with lacy frills around the waist and along the hem up against Felicia. "You'll understand soon enough." She cocked her head one way and then the other and finally smiled and said, "This will be a lovely dress for the party."

But curious Felicia was not to be distracted so easily. "Does Daddy do nasty things to you?" she wanted to know.

Ariel clutched Felicia's hand and hurried them toward the counter. "Only once," she said in a hushed voice. "Only once."

What she said was true. The moment Ariel knew that William had impregnated her, she told him there would be no more of that. Despite the bleak sexual future her words forebode, he followed the guidelines of his stiffly conservative upbringing and married her immediately. After all, her family was far too wealthy to be bought off, and his parents rather liked the idea of his marrying that bright, lovely, wealthy Caruthers girl. They settled into a sprawling home in the Preston Hollow district. When necessary, he sought his physical pleasures elsewhere, behavior she tolerated so long as it was discreet and she could spend and donate his money at will.

William, however, was apparently rather boring in the physical activity department and over the years found fewer and fewer opportunities for elsewhere pleasure. His friends' wives lost interest; his female business associates lost interest; even the household help lost interest.

And so he turned to Jesus. He took his great success in his law practice as a sign that Jesus loved him, and he threw himself into Christianity far more intensely than he had ever thrown himself into physical pleasures. He continued his very lucrative law practice, but at home he generally remained locked in his study, reading the bible, praying, and weeping. Ariel and Felicia rarely saw him, and they ignored him when he did make rare appearances among them.

Felicia remembered her mother's warning. In her late pre-teen years when other girls spoke of some dreamy boy they wished would kiss them, she would shake her head and say, "He will do nasty things to you." As a result, the other girls began to shun her. To compensate for the frequent lack of company, Felicia began avidly reading everything from tomes of history to classic works of fiction and poetry to current events in two or three newspapers every day.

Being intelligent, she remembered everything she read and, in that way, eventually regained access to popularity. During lunch times at school, she would recount famous historical events in a way that charmed the other girls into thinking they were part of those august events. She retold fictions and epic poems in the same way, sometimes, for an especially emphatic effect, placing herself or one of the other girls in the various roles. Her knowledge of history and literature and current events and her ability to convey that knowledge so vividly eventually drew girls and boys alike to her, in large part because she was beautiful and interesting and animated and, perhaps in larger part, because the knowledge she imparted in such a palatable way helped them pass the classes for which their busy social schedules left them little time study.

In this way, Felicia became friends with the high school quarterback during her sophomore year. The boy was—and she recognized this—dumb as the proverbial box of rocks, but he was wealthy and handsome and made her feel things she had never felt before. Her soul went out to him—or, at least, that's how she explained to herself the sensations she felt when she looked at his handsome jaw line or his sleepy brown eyes, or when he said, "Wait, what?" She would scowl at first, but then he would say, "You're so hot, I got distracted. Tell me again about why that guy—what's-his-name—met the devil in the woods." Then she would tell him again, looking intensely into his eyes, and she would feel things in places where she thought her mother might disapprove of having feelings. Thus, she thought of the reaction as her soul reaching out to the boy, something of which, since his family was wealthy, she felt sure her mother would not disapprove.

Once, when they'd had a study session after school, he offered to drive her home. She called her mother who, when she heard the boy's last name, said, "I'm sure that will be fine. Just don't let him dally."

Felicia knew the meaning of the word *dally*, although she wasn't entirely sure of its various specific implications in relation to boys. Thus, when the quarterback said he'd like to stop at a little park he loved, she said that would be fine because she loved little parks and thought they might see something interesting. He parked in an isolated area of the park and said, "Slide over here next to me. I want to show you something." She slid over next to him, feeling tingly and also pleased that this very stupid, handsome, rich young man appreciated nature enough to show her something fascinating. What he showed her was natural enough, she supposed, but it was not something she particularly wanted to see. Then what he tried to do was, she felt quite certain, one of the nasty things to which her mother had referred eight years earlier. She ejected herself from the car immediately. The boy apologized and said he would drive her home. Fearing a second attempt, she declined his offer, opting to walk instead. On her very long walk home, she broke a heel on one of her very upscale shoes ordered from France. Her mother scolded her severely for the broken heel. Felicia accepted her mother's harsh words, apologized, and then explained that the quarterback had attempted to do nasty things to her.

Ariel shuddered and then said, "Never mind about the shoes. We'll get you some new ones. You're a good girl." She patted Felicia's shoulder, looked at her thoughtfully, and then nodded as if she had just made up her mind to say whatever was in it. "You should know, by the way, that if you drink alcohol you are more likely to allow a man to do those things." At her mother's social gatherings, Felicia had observed adults quite enjoying their alcoholic beverages, but it occurred to her now that she had never seen her mother drink anything stronger than carbonated water. Felicia nodded that she understood. They hugged, and they never spoke of the broken heel or the quarterback again.

Felicia made her way through high school and to college without further incident. She continued reading and telling spellbinding stories, still sometimes sprinkling her own appearance into some of them for dramatic effect. She still allowed boys into her audiences, but devoutly avoided any hint of personal interest in them, despite the fact that some quite attracted her and made her tingle. After a time, then, boys lost interest and stopped listening to her stories. For some it meant lower grades in classes, but at least they spent their mixed-gender social inter-action more fruitfully.

What the quarterback had attempted to do, coupled with her avid reading regimen, had instilled in her a solid general notion of what kinds of nasty things boys were capable and were quite eager and willing to do to girls. The specifics as well as the nuances of the mechanics escaped her, and she remained certain, thanks to her mother's warning, that she did not want them done to her. Still, she found that reading about them, mostly via veiled references, often added interest and conflict to a tale, not to men-tion that it sometimes made her tingle in that pleasant way to which she had become accustomed. Sometimes, if the tingling were strong, her eyes did something funny that she couldn't quite identify. They didn't cross exactly, but they cocked in an odd sort of way, and she would have to stop reading until the sensation dissipated and her eyes could again focus on the page. Having become a master story teller or, rather, story re-teller, she decided to add such interest and conflict to her own presentations. The references, of course, never assumed the form of vivid description but were conveyed, rather, by implication, innuendo, and double entendre. They were a smashing hit with her female narratees, particularly when she cast herself as one of the characters.

Even so, gatherings to hear her stories grew smaller as other girls had more and more opportunities to attend frat parties and other similar celebrations. Felicia rarely received invitations, and she declined on those few occasions when she did. The parties, she knew, consisted of high consumption of alcoholic beverages and, to hear other girls tell it, a significant amount of nasty behavior from which she made every effort to distance herself. After a time, she felt rather lonely in college.

Early in her sophomore year, a psychology professor required all students in his class to attend, as observers, a group counseling session of some sort. He randomly assigned a specific group to each student, and she was to visit a grief counseling group that met in the basement of an Episcopal church. A slender man with a shy smile whose shoulders slumped from the weight of his grief greeted her when she arrived. The session had not begun, he explained, but cookies and punch or coffee were available at the table behind him. Despite his droopy shoulders, she judged him rather handsome with his close-cropped dark hair and dark lashes above brilliantly blue eyes. He did not make her tingly, but she found him quite pleasant to look at and, thus, to visit with. His name was Eddie.

As more people gathered, they stood in a corner talking, and when she thought it appropriate she queried as to the source of his grief. "I was madly in love," he said, "with the kindest, gentlest, most beautiful woman in the universe." He paused to wipe a tear from his eye and then continued his tale. He worked as the Assistant Manager of Produce at an H.E.B. store in Richardson, and he had met her when she queried him about how to choose the best avocados. He placed his hand lightly on hers and showed her how to squeeze the fruit gently to determine its readiness. Some time after they became engaged, he was asked to attend a weekend ropes course the store manager had arranged for a select group of employees, and he felt he could not decline. While he learned to work with others at Laity Lodge near Leakey, his fiancée foolishly agreed to have dinner with a friend of her brother's visiting from Oklahoma. Later, riddled with guilt, she confessed to Eddie that they had a fabulous meal and three bottles of wine and then had participated in behavior unbecoming to a betrothed woman. She apologized and begged forgiveness. He told her he wasn't sure he could forgive her. Two days later, he decided he could, but before he got to tell her she died in a fourteen-car pile-up on I-30, drunk and accompanied by her brother's friend from Oklahoma, whose pants were unzipped when the medics pulled his lifeless body from the car.

He wept at the end, and Felicia wept and hugged him. When he wiped his tears away, he said, "So, what about you?"

After the tragic story he had told, she felt she could hardly say she was a student at SMU majoring in—well, in truth she had no major—who had grown up with every advantage wealth afforded and had been traumatized only once by a near-miss with a quarterback. So she said, "My name is Mattie, and two years ago I went to New England to help keep house for my semi-invalid cousin Zeena. I fell madly in love with her husband, Ethan." She modernized the tale where necessary, conveniently omitted the ambiguous nature of Mattie's motivations, and significantly altered the ending so that she survived and poor Ethan was smashed to death against the infamous elm tree.

She wept at the end, and he wept and hugged her.

They sat together during the session, and when it ended he hugged her again and said he looked forward to seeing her the following week. Of course, she did not return the following week.

However, her experience with Eddie impregnated her mind with a notion that she acted upon within two weeks. Eddie had been a kind, gentle man, and he had seemed so damaged and so vulnerable that she felt quite certain he had no desire to do nasty things to women. She reasoned that other such men might be found in other group counseling settings. And so, lonely as she was, she set about finding them. The large number of such gatherings in the metroplex quite surprised her. She avoided those designed to help rape victims and those aimed at rehabilitating sexual predators. But otherwise, she kept an open mind and visited a wide variety of sessions, generally two per week.

Sometimes the meetings were unproductive for her, but at least, she consoled herself, she was getting out for an evening and mingling with others. Other times were very successful, times when she would engage in fascinating conversations with women and men alike, conversations mostly about the nature of their particular problems—hers, of course, gleaned from the tomes of material she had read since junior high school.

In a support group for relatives of schizophrenics, she told of her older brother who believed dogs could talk and even write and who eventually determined that he was the king of Spain. In a support group for relatives of alcoholics, she told of her older brother who drank himself to death in Las Vegas. At others times, she relied on current events of the past few years, altering them just enough to avoid having some clever soul recognize her story.

She did, as she had expected, meet many men who were so otherwise distraught that they seemed to have little interest in the kinds of things men like to do to women. She even went out with one of them

35

occasionally. There was, for example, one named Tom who maintained an unnatural affection for his cats. They went for coffee and had a lovely time until Felicia began sneezing so violently that she could not talk. Assuming—probably correctly—that she was allergic to cat hair, Tom became incensed and stormed out of the coffee shop, leaving her with the bill. Another one, Sidney, whose elderly mother suffered from dementia, took her for ice cream. He was proverbially tall, dark, and handsome, and he made her tingle in that pleasant way. As they visited across a small round table, the sensation became so strong that her eyes did that funny thing, cocking in an odd sort of way, and Sidney began to weep uncontrollably. "Not you," he said to Felicia between sobs. "Not you, too!" He had to excuse himself but was at least gentlemanly enough to leave money for paying the bill.

At some point during her senior year she began to think of Eddie, of his lovely dark hair and beautiful blue eyes, and, though this had not happened when she met him, the memories made her tingle. She returned to the group of which he'd been a member, but a woman there who wore a beret and spoke with a thick French accent said he had been feeling better and did not attend regularly anymore. Felicia drove to Richardson, located the H.E.B. store to which he had referred, and found him misting crispy iceberg lettuce and fat heads of red cabbage. Delighted to see her, he accidentally misted her face when he reached to hug her in greeting. He did, indeed, look better. His shoulders no longer slumped, and his brilliant blue eyes almost sparkled, she thought. Despite her damp face or, perhaps, because of it, she tingled.

They dated for a time, during which he never exhibited any desire to do anything nasty to her. When he proposed, she felt comfortable saying yes. Her parents, quite naturally, reacted negatively to the news that she would wed an assistant manager of produce. Discovering what a pleasant man Eddie was, however, her father thought he might help the young man secure a more lucrative position in the designer vegetable business. Then he made everyone bow their heads in prayer.

When she graduated with a degree in—well, no one was sure what her degree was in, including her—she moved back home and began planning her wedding or, rather, listening to her mother plan her wedding. Ariel suggested the French Riviera for a honeymoon. Having been there several times with her mother, Felicia thought that was a fine idea. When she mentioned it to Eddie, he explained that he simply could not afford such a honeymoon and suggested Corpus Christi instead. She waved him off and observed casually that her parents would be happy to pay. But he remained steadfast, insisting that he would not accept charity. (Later, as they boarded the cruise ship, he also told her he would not accept her father's assistance in getting a job in the designer vegetable trade.) Being a tender soul, Felicia relented but suggested a Caribbean cruise as a compromise. Eddie balked, she pleaded, and he went home to calculate costs. She was pleased the next day when he said he could manage the cruise though he still liked the idea of Corpus better.

The wedding was huge and elegant and beautiful, and the following morning Felicia and Eddie flew to Miami to board their cruise ship. On the third day of the cruise, Felicia reported Eddie missing.

How long had he been missing? the man she reported to wanted to know.

She said two days.

Why had she waited so long to report it? the man wondered.

She'd been seasick, she said, and had opted to stay in the room that first morning when Eddie went for breakfast. He said he might stop after eating to drop a few nickels in the slots. She claimed to have slept most of that day except when she ran to the bathroom to vomit. When she awoke near dark, she assumed Eddie had been lucky at the slots, stayed all day, and then had gone to supper. When she awoke at two a.m., she assumed he had gone to the late-night comedy show. And when she awoke again at eight or so, she assumed he had, perhaps, sat on the deck watching the ocean go by until it was again time for breakfast. She felt better by five or so that afternoon and went looking for him. Not finding him, she finally reported him missing.

The man seemed suspicious, but he nodded and took notes, and ordered a thorough search of the ship. No one found any trace of Eddie, although someone found ten or twelve nickels near the railing on the starboard side of the lido deck. The Coast Guard was called and a helicopter search was conducted from Miami to St. Thomas. No sign of Eddie was found. He was declared lost at sea. Authorities questioned Felicia at length on several occasions but finally said she was free to go. After she signed a waiver agreeing not to sue the cruise line, she flew home at the line's expense and a couple of weeks later received a refund check for the cost of the cruise minus a twenty percent handling fee. Her father said Jesus would punish them for stealing her—or, rather—Eddie's money. Her mother, who had signed no waiver, wanted to sue. Felicia, however, begged her not to, observing that she did not want a drawn-out lawsuit that constantly reminded her of her terrible misfortune, not to mention Eddie's.

Despite her terrible misfortune, her mother insisted they have a heart-to-heart talk and asked if, during the two nights they spent together, Eddie had done nasty things to her.

"Certainly not," Felicia said.

"Well," Ariel said, "did he try?"

"Let's talk about something else, Mother. Did you know that Julia Tuttle was the mother of Miami?"

"But, Sweetheart—"

"Miami was named after a river, but the river was named after the Mayaimi Indians."

"I see," Ariel said, and, despite Felicia's terrible misfortune, changed the subject to thank-you notes. She insisted that Felicia write thank-you notes to the several hundred folk who had given wedding gifts. Felicia stayed in her room for five days straight writing the notes. For five more days after that, all she said, no matter the occasion, was "Thank you." Her mother might say, "Sweetheart, you remember old Mr. Craghart, don't you? Do you know that a twenty-six year old bimbo agreed to marry him!" to which Felicia would reply, "Thank you." Or her mother might say, "Well, my goodness, the Darlings are moving to Los Angeles of all places!" to which Felicia would reply, "Thank you. Thank you, thank you, thank you."

Finally, Ariel pointed out this odd behavior to Felicia, to which Felicia responded, "Thank you." Then, blushing, she said, "I'm sorry. I'll try not to."

Now conscious of her odd speech behavior, she concentrated on saying something other than thank you. Still, her responses often weren't appropriate to the occasion. Her mother might say, "Shall I have Rosita prepare glazed lamb chops or chicken cordon bleu for dinner?" And Felicia might reply, "When I first met Mr. Lamb, I thought him quite handsome."

"What, Dear?" Ariel would query.

"But he was fast friends with Mr. Coleridge, you know, whom I could not abide. So egotistical, so morose at times, and really quite boring, not to mention that he pinched my bottom when no one was looking."

"Felicia, what are you talking about?"

"Dinner, Mother. I'm talking about dinner."

When Ariel would point out that she had not, in fact, been talking about dinner at all, but, rather, about some awful man named Coleridge, Felicia would say, "Oh, I'm sorry. Thank you. Thank you. I believe I would prefer the chicken. Thank you."

And so forth.

Such occasions became so frequent that Ariel decided something must be done. Certain that no one in her family could ever suffer from psychological distress, she determined that Felicia simply had a little speech impediment. Having just made a rather large donation to Dr. Albert Crane Farnsworth's Tell It to Me Slowly Center, she arranged for Felicia's enrollment in the clinic's Group Therapy for Overcoming Verbal Tics. Dr. Farnsworth, after reading *The Reluctant King: The Life and Reign of George VI, 1895-1952*, had made a sizable fortune in his first venture, the Farnsworth Enunciation Clinic for Elite Socialites. Recently, having read a cutting-edge article by Dr. Melinda Floyd-Hendricks in the *International Journal of Language and Communication Disorders*, he had opened the Tell It to Me Slowly Center in a remodeled building adjacent to his FECES clinic.

It was there that Felicia met the harelip—that is, the gentleman with the cleft lip who spoke quite clearly except when he became overly excited about a subject. And he always became overly excited when he spoke of Dr. Melinda Floyd-Hendricks' Speak Up Center in South Carolina. His speech, he said, had been severely impeded by his cleft lip, and when he read in *Time* about the miracles that Dr. Melinda Floyd-Hendricks' Speak Up Center could work, he left Arlington and drove non-stop to get there. The center had, indeed, worked miracles for him, his impediment now surfacing only when he became excited and spoke too fast. Considering his speech significantly rehabilitated and feeling quite homesick, he returned to Arlington and enrolled at the Tell It to Me Slowly

39

Center in hopes of learning to control his excited speech.

There, Felicia had made no progress, had, in fact, regressed a bit according to Dr. Farnsworth's reports, though of course he viewed her regression as a precursor to a huge and miraculous breakthrough she would soon experience. When she began at the center, she might say to someone, "When I first met Napoleon I thought him an odd little man, but he certainly knew a thing or two about how to treat a woman." Then she would pause, breathe deeply, concentrate intensely, and say, "No, what I meant to say is that it's very nice to meet you." Over time, however, the pauses did not work as well. She might say, "My relationship with Rodolphe was quite complicated, but we had such beautiful times together." Then, after the pause and the breathing and the concentration, she might say, "No, what I meant to say is that the most beautiful man I ever met was a very large dead man who washed up on the shores of a little village in South America where I lived for a time." And she seemed never to realize that she had not said, "Yes, it is quite a beautiful day," as she had intended.

Despite his cleft lip, Felicia found the man who spoke of the Speak Up Center rather attractive, and she tingled a bit when they visited. His name was Rupert and he worked at a Dodge service center in Arlington and spent every dime he saved on speech therapy. One day, after a lengthy description of the extravagant dinner parties Jean Des Esseintes gave before he retreated to a reclusive life in the country, she somehow managed to convey that Rupert was invited to dinner at her home or, rather, her parents' home.

Ariel was not especially pleased to have a harelip auto mechanic dining there, but she humored Felicia as much as possible in hopes that her kindness would help her daughter overcome her speech impediment. When Rupert spoke excitedly about the Speak Up Center, some of the words were lost in his throat or nose—Ariel wasn't sure which, but she clearly understood the message and decided to send Felicia there.

So now—finally, you're probably thinking—we get to how Felicia Marie Winstock happened to meet Daniel Alldon at the Speak Up Center in South Carolina and why she spoke to him of Jesus washing her feet.

Once a week at the center, Dr. Melinda Floyd-Hendricks held a recital of sorts in which her clients read or recited or otherwise presented their progress to friends and family invited to the gathering. It was a round robin sort of arrangement. Visitors would move from table to table as Dr. Floyd Hendricks directed so that they ultimately heard all of the clients. Daniel came because of a tongueless in-law there. When he first moved to Felicia's table, she felt the tingle immediately, the strongest tingle, she was quite sure, she had ever experienced. She meant to be bold and direct with him and tell him that he quite captivated her. Instead, she spoke of being kidnapped in France. He seemed, too, to be quite captivated by her and did not want to move to the next table.

She eagerly anticipated his visit the following week and, sure enough, he appeared. She meant to tell him that his eyes were like the ocean but instead told of her terrible misfortune at sea during her honeymoon cruise. She meant to tell him how much she enjoyed their last visit but instead spoke of gluing noodles into the Last Supper for an art project in junior high. The tingling was so strong that for the first time in her life she thought she might actually want a man—this man—to do the nasty things to her that her mother had spoken of so many years before.

On Daniel's third and, unbeknownst to Felicia, last visit, she tingled so intensely that her eyes did that googly thing so that she could not quite see him clearly, but she could certainly feel his presence with every pore of her body. She told him, she thought, how she felt and what she wanted him to do to her. But, alas, what she actually told him was about Jesus washing her feet and the less well known story of his washing the rest of her body as well. Before leaving, he begged her not to be insane, which she took to mean she should not go crazy in his absence because he would return. Yes, she knew he felt what she felt and would return and take her away and do things to her she had only read about but was ready, now, to have done to her.

Dr. Melinda Floyd-Hendricks patted her back and asked how the session had gone. Felicia turned to face her and said, "He was married, you know, and so was I when I first met him. But I was vacationing in Yalta alone, except for the company of my sweet little dog. I never imagined the passion I would come to feel for Gurov nor the passion he would shower on me." She smiled, quite proud of herself for being brave enough to confess to the good doctor the illicit but beautiful relationship she had established with Daniel.

Memory Photos

The day before my mother's memorial service, I arrived late afternoon at our old house in Norman. I had driven from Flagstaff, but got away late the previous day and so stayed over night in Albuquerque. The door was unlocked, so I pushed it open and stepped in. Lacy stood across the room by a knick-knack shelf, a cup of coffee in one hand, a little angel figurine in the other.

"Lacy," I said.

"David," she said.

She wore faded blue jeans and a white, button-up blouse with the sleeves rolled up and the long tail untucked. She had applied no make-up and had pulled her rich, dark hair into a ponytail. She looked to me like the proverbial girl next door. Only she was a woman and she wasn't from next door. She was my sister, whom I had neither seen nor spoken to in almost eleven years.

I dropped my small duffle by the door. "You look good," I said.

"And you." She sipped the coffee. "Should we hug?"

I offered a weak smile. "Maybe not."

She had been born exactly twenty months after I was. In later years our mother never tired of telling about how, even at my young age—before, she would emphasize, I could even speak complete sentences—I coddled baby Lacy. If Lacy cried, Mother said, and couldn't be pacified by feeding or changing, I was the only one who could calm her. I would toddle near and lay my palm against her cheek or arm or tummy or leg, and she would calm immediately.

"Hey," she said. She set her coffee cup on the shelf and picked up a second figurine. She held both up, glass angels with sparkly wings. "Remember these?"

I nodded. "The last birthday present Dad gave her before he died."

Our dad worked for the power company. When I was six and Lacy was almost five, he and two others were electrocuted while trying to restore power to half the city after a hellacious thunderstorm.

"Actually," Lacy said, "we gave them to her. Remember, he had us present them. He said they represented Mom's two angels, you and me."

I snorted. "Some angels, huh?"

"We weren't so bad, David. Not back then. God knows, you were an angel to me."

After Dad died, Lacy tried to be strong, but she was prone to crying at bed time. I would listen from the room next door, fists clenched, body tense, fighting back tears myself. Then Mom would call to me and I'd dash to Lacy's room. "She won't stop," Mom would say, constantly on the verge of tears herself. "She just won't stop." I'd climb up beside Lacy, worm my arm around her shoulders, and with my free hand rub her arm or her leg. The magic didn't work as quickly as when she was an infant, but she would slowly begin to calm and would eventually stop crying. Often, we fell asleep that way, her little head cradled on my little shoulder. She would ease into sleep, and I would watch her stomach rise and fall gently with her breathing until my eyes, too, drifted closed.

Lacy looked at the angels one more time, then set them back gently on the shelf. "Actually," she said, "we *aren't* that bad. We were never *that* bad." She picked up the coffee cup, its contents cold by then, I was sure. She stared down into it. "Life happens, you know? Things happen. My friend Portia taught me that."

I laughed. "You have a friend named Porsche? Like the car?"

She chuckled. "Same sound, different spelling. She's beautiful and she's lesbian. That's why she says things happen."

"And you?"

She shook her head. "Tried. Turns out, you can't just make yourself lesbian."

"Men?"

"Nothing major. You?"

"Turns out," I said, "I'm not so good at long-term relationships."

"Yeah. Things happen."

"Let's talk about something else."

44

She nodded and scanned the shelves, probably searching for another topic of conversation, something simple, something neutral. I had nothing. I looked at my feet. "Aunt Nancy's been great," Lacy finally said.

Aunt Nancy, Mom's sister, had called when Mom died. She had already thought of everything but didn't want to make any arrangements without our permission. I couldn't get away for a day or two and offered blanket permission. Apparently Lacy had, too.

"She planned everything, made all the arrangements," Lacy added. "She's great."

"Arranged the cremation, the service, everything."

"Yeah," I said. "I know."

"Of course," she said apologetically. She took a couple short steps away from the shelves. "You want coffee?" She headed toward the kitchen.

I followed. "Maybe a cola."

I opened a cabinet where I knew glasses would be, pulled out a tall one. Lacy opened the refrigerator. The kitchen smelled familiar, and when I turned toward Lacy the scene looked familiar as well. How many times had I seen her bent in front of the refrigerator searching for something. I would watch until she straightened with whatever prize she had found to satisfy whatever craving she had.

I would have sworn that Lacy's blue-jeaned butt looked no different than it had twelve or fourteen years ago. She found a soda, stepped to the counter. I pulled a few ice cubes from the freezer, dropped them into my glass. "A little bourbon with that?" she asked. She popped open the can.

"No thanks," I said. "Haven't had drink since graduation night." I meant college graduation, and she knew it.

"Very noble."

I shook my head. "Nothing noble. Just thought it would help."

"Has it?"

"Not much."

I set my glass on the counter, and she poured until the foam ran over the top. I reached for a sponge in the sink, wiped up the mess while she downed the remains of the can. I dropped the sponge back into the sink.

She laid a tentative hand on my shoulder. "Nothing does, does it?"

Spontaneously, I reached for her arm, cupped it just above her elbow. Her skin felt just the same as I remembered: soft and smooth and warm to the touch. I released her elbow and stepped aside so that her hand fell from my shoulder.

I had always loved the feel of Lacy's skin. In grade school, whenever something upset her or made her sad, I'd revert to the old method, rubbing her arm or sometimes her leg. It eased her mind, and it eased mine as well.

I sipped my soda, and she stared hard at me.

"So," she said, "why'd you go? Why'd you leave after graduation?"

"I was drunk."

"No," she said. "You were pusillanimous."

I arched my eyebrows, grinned despite feeling uncomfortable. "Big word," I said.

She tapped her temple with a long, slender index finger. "Smart girl."

And she was, had always been.

Because of that and because of when her birthday fell, she began school earlier than most, just a year behind me. She was quick and bright and charming, and by the end of her third-grade year her teacher recommended she take the tests to skip a grade. She took the tests, Mom filled out the paperwork, and when I hit fifth grade, so did she. That year, Mom said we were too old for me to rub her cheek or arm or legs. I stopped, but I still occasionally and casually brushed against Lacy whenever I could. She always smiled, fully aware of my purpose.

Lacy opened a cabinet under the sink, dropped the empty soda can into the trash. "Hey," she said, "want to look at some old pictures of Mom?"

"Sure."

Spontaneously, she grabbed my hand as if to pull me into the living room. I flinched. My inclination was to pull out of her grip, but her hand felt warm, comforting, so I didn't resist. Once during our seventh-grade year, Mom went on the third and last date she ever attempted after Dad died. Lacy and I stayed home alone. I fixed popcorn while Lacy plopped on the couch and flicked on some made-for-tv-movie about a boy who badly missed his father during World War II. I brought the popcorn in, set the bowl next to Lacy's legs, which she had stretched across the coffee table. She wore shorts, so her legs were bare. When I sat down, I casually brushed the back of my hand along one of those long, slender legs. She smiled. When I started to move my hand, she grabbed it and pressed it against her leg. We held hands for the entire movie and didn't speak at all.

The father of the World-War-II-boy was overseas, and the boy missed and worried about him terribly. As a result, he became a bit of a trouble-maker. His mother had quite the time controlling him, as did his teachers. But in the end, his father, though missing an arm, returned home alive to tears and laughter and hugs. I'm sure Lacy and I both wished our father could return that way, but our hand-holding eased us both enough that the movie's end caused no tears. As the movie credits flashed across the screen, we became self-conscious about holding hands. We disengaged and never mentioned the incident later.

In the living room the day before our mother's memorial service, Lacy released my hand in order to pull some photo albums off a shelf. She plopped them onto the scuffed coffee table, sat down, patted the spot next to her. I sat. She selected an album, ran her palm over the faded red cover, then flipped it open.

"Sure you won't be bored?" she asked.

"I won't. I like photos."

"That's right, you really did open that camera shop, didn't you?"

In Flagstaff, I eked out a living from a little camera shop/art studio. Mostly, I sold disposables and cheap digitals to tourists, but occasionally a serious shopper bought a real camera or maybe one of my own photographs from the studio. Lacy lived in Miami, where she made a killing in real estate.

"Yeah," I said. "But without your business savvy it's not all that successful."

She looked down at the first page in the album. "Who's fault is that?"

"I'm guessing you'll say mine."

"Do you disagree?"

I shrugged, a gesture she missed, intent as she was on studying the album and avoiding eye contact.

Lacy and I both wanted to move away from Norman for college, but we—and Mom—couldn't afford out-of-state tuition. So we enrolled at Oklahoma State University in Stillwater. During the first two years, we took as many core courses together as possible. Studying together got me through math and science courses, her through humanities courses. She majored in business management, I in art. Charcoal was my favorite medium until I took a photography course, and from then on the only art I cared about was what I could create through the lens. Our senior year we cooked up a scheme to open a camera shop together. My knowledge of and abilities with cameras and her sharp business sense and smooth people skills would make us a fortune, we were sure. We'd start small, we agreed, but over time we'd expand until we owned three or four stores and an art studio featuring mostly photography. She wanted our business to be in Florida. I didn't care as long as it wasn't Oklahoma. We were naïve, but we were enthusiastic and absolutely confident.

The day before graduation, I gave her a large hanging basket of purple petunias. She liked other flowers better, but the petunias were cheaper. "Keep them alive," I beamed. "We'll hang them outside our shop."

I left two days later, and neither of us ever saw those petunias hanging outside a co-owned business.

Lacy and I took our time looking over the photos in the album she had opened, each of us occasionally making some innocuous observation about a picture. It was not nostalgic, just something to pass the time without too much discomfort.

Toward the end of the album were a couple of pages of separate photos of us decked out for senior prom. In one of her, she stood with a tall, skinny boy, his arm slipped around her waist, grinning from ear-to-ear. She tapped a fingernail on his image and chuckled softly. "You broke that guy's nose, remember?"

"Sorry," I said.

"You kidding? I was forever a grateful. What a dick he was!"

At the dance, he had gotten a little too handsy. I had stepped away from my partner, pulled the two of them apart, and popped him straight in the nose for those few seconds of pleasure he might have received for fondling my sister's ass during a slow dance. He made no attempt to retaliate, just cursed me violently and walked away. I took Lacy home, dropping off my date along the way.

Lacy closed the album and again ran her palm over the red cover. "Mom said she picked this album because of my dress."

"It was a beautiful dress," I said, and suddenly an unbidden memory flooded me, a memory of a moment before the prom.

When we lived at home, our rooms were our own, but neither of us barred the other or bothered with the formality of knocking. The evening of our senior prom, we both had dates that didn't excite us much. On my way out to pick up the girl, I stopped at Lacy's door to tell her I was leaving and would see her there. I pushed open the door and saw her standing in front of her full-length mirror adjusting her dress. It was short and tight and red, with a v-neck that revealed just a hint of cleavage. She wore red heels to match.

"God," I said.

She looked around. "What's wrong?" Her chestnut hair tumbled over her shoulders in wavy curls created just for this night.

"Nothing." I stared at her. "You just look so great."

She dipped her head. "Thanks."

"Really beautiful," I said. "So prepossessing."

She stepped over to straighten my tie. "Big word," she said.

I tapped my temple with my index finger. "Smart guy," I said.

She fiddled with the knot and studied my face. She smiled, her full lips red like her dress and heels. "Right. And not too bad looking either." The smile was closed-lipped and looked a little wistful.

I kissed her. Just a light kiss, a peck on her lips. She pulled back, studied my face again, then leaned in and returned the favor. I folded my arms around her and pulled her into a tight hug. She gripped my sides, pressed her cheek against mine. Her hair smelled of the lavender shampoo she used, her neck of Chanel, a prom gift from Mom. I kissed her again, but stronger this time, and then she parted her lips and we indulged in a full-on, deep, open-mouthed kiss. Fully engaged as she was in the kiss, she still managed, after a moment, to press her palms against my chest and gently push me away.

"We can't," she said. "It's wrong."

"Lacy." I reached to take her hand, but she turned her back before I could.

49

"It's wrong." She raised her hands to her face and I thought maybe she was crying.

"Right," I said. "I'll go."

In the living room, Lacy didn't reach for another photo album. She sat quietly for a time and then stretched affectedly. "I'm really beat," she said. "Think I'll turn in early." Neither of us had eaten, and it was still very early evening, maybe seven. "I took my old room. Assume you'll take yours."

"Sounds fine."

"Okay," she said, rising. "Service is at ten tomorrow."

"Got it," I said.

"Good night."

"Good night."

The last time I had said goodnight to Lacy was eleven years before, the night of college graduation. Mom had come up early that day to visit but left right after the ceremony. She always hated spending a night away from home. That night, Lacy and I attended a graduation bash. Neither of us had any particularly close friends, but we knew plenty of people and enjoyed reminiscing about the previous four years, saying our goodbyes, and getting thoroughly drunk.

Against my better judgment, I got behind the wheel and drove Lacy to her apartment complex. Apparently more thoroughly drunk than I, she stumbled getting out of the car and thunked against the asphalt of the parking lot. I went around and pulled her to her feet. She was laughing. We made our stumbling way to her apartment, she leaning heavily against me, my arm around her to hold her up. Inside, she slumped into her bedroom, kicked off her shoes, and dropped onto the bed.

"Goodnight," I said. "See you tomorrow."

"Stay," she said.

"I better go."

"Come on, David. Just till I fall asleep. God, I'll be passed out in two minutes."

I walked to the other side of the bed. I didn't dare lie down for fear I'd be passed out in two minutes as well. Lacy smiled a lopsided smile, her eyes closed, hair disheveled.

"Hey," she said. "'member after Daddy died? How you'd lie next to me? How you'd cradle my head on your shoulder and rub my arm?" She raised her arm, bare up to the cuff of her half-sleeve. "Or my leg." She attempted to raise her leg, clothed in jeans, but her alcohol-saturated muscles couldn't manage. "Or my tummy." She pulled her blouse far enough up to reveal her flat, soft stomach. "Do it now," she said. "Please."

"Probably a bad idea," I said.

"Please. Just for old times' sake. Just for a minute."

Despite the sanity I'd previously mustered through my alcoholic haze, her pleading and the image of the two of us snuggled together while she fell asleep overcame me. I lay back beside her and inched my arm under her neck. She snuggled her head against my shoulder. I eased my other palm onto her bare stomach, gently caressed her skin. She purred. Her breath was warm—hot, maybe—against my neck. And then her lips were there, just brushing my neck at first, then kissing lightly. She raised her head, kissed my jaw line. I slipped my hand onto her bra, squeezed her breast. She moaned, then pushed herself up and rolled on top of me, her hips straddling mine. She leaned down, kissed me fully on the lips. She unbuttoned my shirt, kissed my chest. I reached for her bra strap but bumbled and didn't manage to unsnap it. She went for my belt buckle, undid it, and then fumbled to unbutton my jeans. Somehow, totally lost as I was in her, an image of little Lacy flashed through my head, little Lacy falling asleep on my shoulder while I watched the rise and fall of her tummy as her breathing slowed.

I clutched her hands, pulled them away from my waist, kissed her knuckles. "We can't," I said.

"David."

"It's wrong."

She sighed. "Right," she said. She rolled onto her stomach and buried her face in a pillow. I stood up and buttoned my shirt. "Goodnight, Lacy." She didn't answer, disappointed, perhaps, or embarrassed, or just plain exhausted.

At my own apartment, I slept little, arose at five, and grabbed my duffle from a closet shelf. I stuffed in a few clothes, some cds, necessary toiletries. I left a note: "Sorry. Do whatever you want with my stuff." I threw my duffle in the back seat of my car and drove west, no destination in mind. And I hadn't spoken to Lacy again until, eleven years later, our

Mom died.

After stretching affectedly and announcing how tired she was, she headed upstairs. I wandered around the house for a while, noting the disrepair it had fallen into. Nothing major, just cosmetics. I wondered if we should get some painting done, maybe replace some carpets. But of course, we would sell our childhood home, and new owners could take care of such chores as they wished. I grabbed my duffle, went up to my room, and read until my eyes felt heavy.

The next day, all went smoothly. Before the service, Aunt Nancy asked quite hesitantly if perhaps she could keep the ashes. We said of course. Whatever she had planned for them had to better than anything I had thought of, which was nothing. What, after all, does one do with a mother's ashes?

The service was respectful, and the pastor, who had known Mom for most of their adult lives, inspired both laughter and tears. During the reception, Mom's house—our house—was full of laughter and tears as well as people mingled, recalled various memories of Mom, and snacked on the piles of food Aunt Nancy and her friends had provided. Lacy and I mingled, too, Lacy insisting that we speak to every individual there and thank them for attending. Most, we hadn't seen since childhood; some, we'd never met all, including some distant relatives from Texas we had never before heard mentioned.

As the crowd diminished, Aunt Nancy and her crew began clean-up, leaving the house spotless. Aunt Nancy kissed us both and invited us to a light supper of leftover reception snacks whenever we felt like coming. Lacy accepted for both of us. Physically and emotionally spent, we both collapsed onto the couch and sighed simultaneously.

"So," Lacy said.

"So," I said.

We sat in silence for a time, our heads flopped against the couch back. Finally, she sat forward. "Think I'll grab a short nap."

"Good idea."

"An hour, maybe. Then we'll go to Aunt Nancy's."

"About that," I said. "maybe you could offer my regrets. I'd like to get some photos around here. Inside and out. You know, memory photos."

"Sure. She'll understand. Share them with me?"

"Sure."

We went to our separate rooms. I fought off old memories as best I could and dozed a little. Then I rolled off the bed, selected a camera, and slipped the strap around my neck. I passed Lacy's room on the way out. The door was open. Inside, she stood in front of the full-length mirror, dressed in her red prom dress and red heels.

She looked around at me. "It was in the closet. It still fits."

I thought perhaps it fit even more snugly and perhaps rode higher up her thigh, but it did, indeed, more or less fit. "I'm not surprised. You're in great shape. You're beautiful."

She dipped her head. It struck me as a perfect pose, the sexy red dress and heels contrasted with the innocence of the shyly dipped head. I raised my camera and shot. At the sound of the shutter, she looked up, surprised, maybe a little shocked, but after a few-seconds' pause, she grinned a wide, white grin. I shot.

"Hey," she said, "what about this?" She made a pouty face. I shot. She struck a severe looking pose. I shot. She struck a come-hither pose. I shot. She stuck out one hip, placed a hand on it. She bent over, hands on knees, and looked provocatively toward the camera. She sat on the bed, raised one leg, and reached toward the raised foot as if to remove the high heel, which dangled from her toes. She arose, turned sideways to me and looked over her shoulder at the camera.

"I love that one," I said. "How about a little more shoulder?"

She tried, but the dress was tight and the shoulder wouldn't budge. She reached behind her back, slid the zipper down a few inches, then slid the fabric and a red bra strap off her left shoulder. She posed sideways again. I shot a full-length picture, then from the waist up, then just her face and shoulder. I zoomed farther, shot just the shoulder, smooth and creamy-white except for a few small freckles. She slipped the dress off of her right shoulder so that both were revealed, raised the shoulders, and struck a Betty Boop big-eyed pose. I shot and shot and shot.

She looked flushed, her skin radiant. My forehead felt damp, my legs wobbly, but I kept a steady hand and shot without thinking. She was likely not thinking, either, for she was totally absorbed in the process. She went all-out, nothing parsimonious about what she gave to the camera lens, and with that lens I consumed it all, everything she offered. She

53

placed her palm on her sternum just below her breasts, ran her zipper fully down, and let the dress top fall onto her hand and arm. The bra was red, and the dark spots of her nipples showed through the sheer fabric. Again, I snapped a variety of full shots and close-ups, and in a shot of just her chest I noted, on her left breast, a second dark spot above the nipple.

I lowered the camera. "You have a tattoo?"

She grinned and nodded and then unsnapped the bra. Holding the dress in place with one hand and then the other, she slipped the short dress sleeves and bra straps off of her arms. She flung the bra on the bed.

I sucked in my breath at the sight, her breasts not large, but still perky and perfect for her figure. The tattoo was a small purple petunia, blossoming open just above her nipple, as if on the verge of sucking it in.

I raised the camera again and kept shooting. Soon, she let the dress fall and stepped out of it, naked now but for the red high heels and red panties as sheer as the bra. She spread her legs, hands on hips, and arched her back. She turned sideways, one leg raised with her foot on the bed. She sat very erect on the edge of the bed, long legs crossed, hands folded on the top one, looking for all the world like a prim and proper school teacher gone wild. She twisted, lay full-length on the bed, knees raised, heels planted firmly on the bed's surface. She opened the legs and looked down between them. I crouched at the foot of the bed and shot her faced framed by the open legs.

She arose and slipped the panties off slowly. I shot every stage of the process, and then I shot the aftermath in every pose she struck.

Finally, she kicked off the heels. I snapped two shots, then a third and fourth. I stopped.

"God," I said.

She released a long sigh and collapsed onto the bed, her head and shoulders propped against a pile of fat pillows. Her skin was rosy and glistened with perspiration. She breathed heavily, and I watched the rise and fall of her stomach. I, too, felt sweaty and hot and totally spent.

I tried to gather my wits. "So," I said. "It's getting late. You should get to Aunt Nancy's."

"Not tonight. I'll see her tomorrow."

I nodded and slipped the camera strap off my neck.

"You're almost out of light," she said, "for your memory photos."

I rolled my eyes, sighed. "I think I've taken enough photos for the evening."

* * *

Just as I had done that morning after graduation, I left before sunrise while Lacy still slept. I drove straight through to Flagstaff. Exhausted as I was, I still stayed up to download the photos of Lacy from my camera to my computer. I studied them carefully, one-by-one. I selected one to send her, the first one, the one of her in her red dress and heels, her head dipped after I complimented her. I e-mailed her a copy but included no note.

The next day I slept in and decided not to open the shop. I unpacked the few things in my duffle. I opened mail that arrived while I was away, all bills and advertisements. I checked the fridge and pantry, made a grocery list. I drove to the grocery store to purchase what I needed. I stopped at a liquor store and bought a pricey bottle of red wine. I put on sweats and tennis shoes, drove to a nearby park and ran twice around its two-mile jogging trail. Back home I showered. I turned on the tv, watched a documentary about giraffes. I paced. I dusted furniture. I worked a crossword puzzle. I selected a frozen dinner, chicken and potatoes au gratin, and popped it in the microwave. I poured a glass of the pricey wine, my first drink in nearly eleven years. I drank the wine while I ate. The food's texture and taste was cardboard. The wine tasted delicious. I stopped after the one glass. I turned on my computer, intending to delete the photos of Lacy. I looked through them all, then looked through them again. I turned off my computer and went to bed.

Sketchbook

While his fifth-grade classmates bustled out the door for recess, Sebastian moved slower and didn't look up. When only he and Mrs. Klingman remained in the room, she said, "You'd better get going, Sebastian."

"Yes, ma'am." He slid his sketchbook and a pencil off his desk. Outside, he walked slowly around the corner and plopped down in a grassy spot shaded by the building. His back against the wall, he raised his knees and propped the notebook against them. He stared at the blank page for several seconds, then turned the notebook lengthways across his legs. He sketched the long, slender body of an insect and drew lines that segmented it into ten sections. He stopped to study his work so far, tilting his head first to the right and then to the left.

"Hey, Sebastian." He looked up at the pudgy face of Kenny Brower. Kenny panted, his face red and sweaty. "Want to play some football?"

Sebastian looked past Kenny and past the cement pad that served as a basketball court out to the field where a group of boys tossed a football around. He looked back at Kenny. "You want *me* to play?"

Kenny shrugged. "The teams are uneven. My team needs another player." He raised his right arm to wipe his forehead on his sleeve. Sweat rings had already formed in the armpits of the shirt.

"Thanks," Sebastian said, "but I think I'll just keep drawing."

"Come on," Kenny said. "Just for awhile."

"No, I guess not."

"Sissy." Kenny turned to leave, paused, then turned back and in a quicker, smoother movement than his rotund body looked capable of scooped the pencil out of Sebastian's hand. He cracked the pencil in half against his knee and threw the eraser end several yards away. The sharpened end he pressed against the wall until the lead snapped. He sneered and threw the broken stub into Sebastian's lap. "Pussy!" He trotted away, his belly jiggling with every step.

Sebastian held the pencil piece up and picked at it with his fingernail. A few splinters of wood chipped away, but not enough to reveal the lead. He tried again, but no other splinters broke away.

"You picked a nice shady spot," a woman's voice said, and hearing it, he blushed immediately.

He glanced up at her and then quickly away. "Yes, ma'am."

* * *

Three weeks before the end of the school year, Mrs. Duncan, the other fifth-grade teacher, had taken a leave to care for her husband, who had had back surgery. Ms. Freeman, who had just graduated from college the previous December, stepped in to finish out the year. She had started that Monday, and on Tuesday Sebastian had run into her—literally. As he headed down the hall to his classroom that morning, she walked several steps ahead of him. Just before he reached his room, Kenny Brower slipped in behind him and pushed hard against his back. He stumbled forward and flung his arms up to keep from smashing his face against Ms. Freeman's back. His palms landed firmly against her butt and made her stumble forward as well. When they both caught their balance, Kenny was nowhere in sight.

Sebastian's face burned. "I'm sorry," he said and side-stepped her to make a quick getaway. But she laid a hand on his shoulder to stop him. She didn't grab and she didn't clutch. She simply rested her palm gently on the shoulder.

"Are you okay?" she asked. He stared at his feet, nodded. "You got pushed, didn't you?"

"I tripped," he said. "I'm sorry."

She moved her hand from his shoulder, cupped his chin with her soft, warm palm, and tilted his head up so that he had to look at her. Her red hair tumbled in waves and curls over her shoulders. She had green eyes, and her smile, a kind, sympathetic smile, revealed perfectly straight, very white teeth. "Are you sure?"

He tried to look away, but she held his chin. "Yes ma'am. I tripped.

I'm sorry."

She studied his face, then released his chin. "Well," she said, "don't you worry about it. You should see me. I'm such a klutz, I trip all the time. Don't you worry about it, okay?"

"Okay," he said. "Yes ma'am. Thank you." And he made his escape.

At the end of that school day, he was almost to the bicycle rack when Kenny Brower, followed closely by David Hatch, caught up to him. "So," Kenny said, "did you cop a good feel?"

Sebastian kept walking toward his bicycle and didn't look around at Kenny. "Leave me alone."

"What's the matter, didn't you like feeling up a teacher's butt?"

"Shut up."

"Did she like it? Did she like you squeezing her butt? Did she moan?"

Sebastian whirled, ducked his shoulder, and lunged at Kenny's gut. Kenny dodged and Sebastian's shoulder just swished air. He spun toward Kenny. "Shut up about her," he said. "Just leave me alone." He trotted the few steps to his bike. As he mounted, Kenny and David laughed and slapped each other's backs. He rode away.

* * *

And now, two days later, here she was, observing that he had picked a nice shady spot to sit.

He glanced up at her and then quickly away. "Yes, ma'am."

"Mind if I join you?" She didn't wait for an answer, instead easing down onto the grass beside him, her knees pulled up like his. Her long, loose white dress tented over her legs and covered everything except the tips of her sandals and toes, which were also the only parts of her poking beyond the shade line and into the sun. She wore clear polish on her toes, so that the nails glinted in the light. "I like your drawing," she said and tapped the notebook page with her forefinger, the nail of which was also painted with clear, shiny polish. "Is it a dragonfly?"

Sebastian nodded. "Yes, ma'am. Or it will be when I'm finished."

She laughed and eased the pencil stub out of his hand. "It doesn't look like you'll be finishing with this."

"I guess not."

"Who did this?"

"It was an accident."

"It's a lot of damage for an accident."

"Yes, ma'am, I guess so."

"Well," she said, "I want you to finish that drawing." She pushed her fingers into a mass of red curls and slid a pencil out from behind her ear. "So I better give you this."

He reached for the pencil but still avoided eye-contact. "Thank you."

"But if you use my pencil," she said, "you have to show me the finished drawing."

Sebastian studied his partial drawing again. He nodded. "Okay. Yes, ma'am."

She patted his shoulder. "Don't forget." She smiled and pushed up onto her feet. A couple of small blades of grass clung to her dress right where his hands had landed two days before. He almost spoke, but finally looked away instead.

He considered the segmented dragonfly body briefly and then flipped to a blank page. He drew a long, wavy line and then another and another until together they began to look like a thick head of hair around an invisible face. He filled half the page with them, adding curls and ringlets like Ms. Freeman's that created a rich fullness on the page. He tilted his head left and right, occasionally adding a little shading here and there. He drew the eyebrows, thin and slightly arched, and then began on the eyes. He worked slowly, carefully shaping and shading to reflect the same depth and warmth of her sparkling green ones. He had not quite finished the second eye when the bell rang and students, some making noises of disappointment, stopped whatever they were doing and began filing into the building. Teachers clapped their hands and called to those who lagged behind, including the boys playing football.

Ms. Freeman walked with two girls from her class, one on each side of her. She spoke to them, and they listened intently and smiled. When they neared Sebastian, he flipped his notebook closed and joined the line. "Did you finish?" Ms. Freeman asked. She looked down at the girls and said, "He's quite an artist, you know." He blushed. The girls rolled their eyes and giggled. "Let's see it," Ms. Freeman said to him. "Show us your dragonfly."

"It's not quite finished. I'd rather wait."

"Okay," she said. "But don't forget."

"No, ma'am, I won't."

* * *

That evening at home, Sebastian wandered into his older sister's room, his hands shoved deep in his pockets. Fifteen and star-struck, his sister lay crossways, stomach-down, on her bed. Propped up on her elbows, she leafed through a teen magazine. "What do you want?" she asked without looking away from the magazine.

"Nothing." He leaned against the door frame. "I was just wondering something."

"Aren't we all." She turned a page. "Like I'm wondering when he'll marry me." She stared at a full-page photograph of a teenage boy wearing jeans but no shirt. Strands of his unkempt hair fell across his eyes. Thumbs hooked in his jeans' pockets, he slouched against a wall and smirked at the camera. His eyelids were half closed, but the eyes themselves seemed to stare straight off the page. Sebastian's sister leaned her head down and kissed the photograph right where the boy's lips were. She looked up. "Stop gawking," she said. "What do you want?"

"Nothing," he said. "Never mind."

Back in his own room, he sat at his desk, where his sketchbook was opened to the drawing of Ms. Freeman's hair and eyebrows and eyes, which he had finished earlier in the evening. He left her noseless and began forming the shape of her lips. Their fullness was, perhaps, a bit exaggerated, but rather than correct the error he worked on light shading he hoped would create the illusion of the satiny sheen of her clear lip gloss.

Satisfied, he laid his pencil down and ran his fingertips across the lips, lightly so as not to smudge them. He closed his eyes, raised his hand from the page, and pressed the fingertips against his own lips.

* * *

The next day, Friday, because he hadn't finished the dragonfly, Sebastian kept a careful watch and avoided any meetings with Ms. Freeman. Over the weekend, he finished his first drawing of her and began another, one in which she smiled brightly, her arms wrapped around her raised knees, the long, loose dress tenting her legs and covering everything but the tips of her sandals and toes. The following Monday, he finished the dragonfly, and on Tuesday he arrived a little early for school and watched for Ms. Freeman's arrival.

That day, she wore black slacks and a tucked-in tan blouse with swooping black swirls of varying sizes. He waited until she entered the building, and by the time he arrived at her room, she already sat at her desk entering math quiz grades in her grade book. She stopped her work immediately when he paused in the open doorway.

"Good morning, Sebastian." She smiled broadly, exposing those bright white teeth. "Come on in. I've been wanting to see your drawing."

"I brought it," he said. "And I brought your pencil back." He stepped to her desk, laid the pencil next to her grade book, and opened his sketchbook to the dragonfly page.

She studied the drawing closely, then said, "That's amazing. You really are very good. It looks exactly like a dragonfly."

He blushed. "I like them. Dragonflies, I mean. And other bugs, too. I think it's about right."

She looked at the drawing again. "I like bugs, too. They're fascinating creatures. And this dragonfly isn't about right, it's exactly right." She placed her thumb at the bottom of the page as if to turn it. "What else have you drawn?"

He quickly slipped the book off her desk. "They're not finished."

She laughed and patted his back. "All right. But you show me when you're finished, okay?"

"Yes, ma'am."

"Oh, and—" She picked up the pencil he had left by her grade book. " you'd better keep this."

"Yes, ma'am. Thank you." He gripped the pencil in his fist and left, still blushing.

They did not cross paths for a couple of days, but Sebastian placed himself strategically so that he could watch her arrive at school, interact with teachers and students during recess, or walk to her Toyota Corolla and slide gracefully into the driver's seat at the end of the day. He drew a picture of her at her desk, pencil in hand, thick, curly hair tumbling onto her grade book. The swooping black swirls of varying sizes on her blouse appeared to be silhouettes of the curls in her hair.

On Friday, she joined him again in the shade of the building during recess. She talked about art. She talked about insects. She talked about places she'd traveled with college-sponsored groups. She described the strange Orchid Mantis she had seen in Malaysia and the amazingly strong Hercules Beetle that crossed her path on a hike in South America. She made him promise he would draw them just as she described.

The next week, the last week of school, was filled with activities, most of them fun, some of them designed to review students over course material. And Sebastian continued to watch Ms. Freeman whenever he had the chance.

At the end of the day Thursday, he spotted Kenny Brower and David Hatch running away from the bike rack as he approached. Both his tires were flat. He lifted the back end of the bike and spun the tire looking for slashes or punctures, but he found none. The same was true of the front tire. They had simply let all the air out. He sat underneath a nearby oak tree and jerked his sketchbook from his backpack. He angrily erased several segments of the dragonfly's tail and then redrew it so that it curved up over the insect's back, and he added a scorpion-like stinger at the end. He erased portions of the front two legs and drew small, pointed talons there. He erased the mouth area and redrew it so that it appeared to grimace, revealing a row of razor-sharp teeth. Immersed in the work, he did not hear Ms. Freeman approaching, and she stood over him before he knew she was there.

"That's a scary-looking creature," she said.

He shrugged. "I was just imagining."

"Well, I hope you don't imagine it to life." She laughed and added, "Although parts of it do look like a scorpion fly."

"I've never seen one. But I have read about them. They're harmless to people, I think."

"Yes," she said. "I believe you're right."

"Yeah, he probably is too." Sebastian tapped the eraser end of his pencil against the wicked-looking dragonfly. "He looks mean, but he's probably not."

She squatted next to him. "So why are you drawing out here in this heat instead of at home where it's nice and cool."

"I just felt like it."

She nodded toward his bike. "Do those flat tires have anything to do with it?"

"Not really. I'll walk it home. It's not far."

"How did that happen?"

He shrugged.

"Did someone do that?"

"I didn't see anybody do it. It's okay. I have a pump at home."

"Let me give you a ride. It's awful hot."

"Okay," he said. "Thank you."

He pushed his bike behind her, watching the hem of her bright blue skirt sway around her calves. When they arrived at the car, she opened the trunk. "I better just push it home," he said. "The trunk's pretty small."

"Not to worry," she said. "Watch this."

She rolled the bike out of his hands, grabbed the frame, lifted, and nestled it perfectly into the trunk. "See," she grinned. "Anything you want to do is possible if you think about how to do it."

In the car, she waved her hand in front of her face. "Wow, it's hot." She pushed her mid-length sleeves as far up her arms as they would go. She pulled the hem of her skirt back slightly, just above her knees. "Let's get it cooled down." She started the engine and twisted the air-conditioner control knob to high. He gave her directions, and during the short drive she spoke of how much she had enjoyed teaching during the last three weeks. She said she had applied for a full-time position and sure hoped she'd get it. He watched her jaw line as she spoke, her lips, her white teeth, her thick, curly red hair.

"Maybe," he said, "if you don't get it you could teach at the middle school."

"Maybe. I am certified for middle school, too. But I'd rather teach fourth or fifth grade."

"Yeah," he said. "But still . . ."

She smiled at him. "But still . . ." she agreed.

At his house, she popped the trunk and he wrestled the bike out. He rolled it up next to her window, which she rolled down. "Thanks again, Ms. Freeman."

"My pleasure, Sebastian. I always enjoy talking with you."

"Yes, ma'am. Me too."

His face reddened and he quickly turned and pushed his bike toward the garage. "See you at the class party tomorrow," she called after him.

"Yes, ma'am." He raised his hand in a wave but did not look back.

* * *

The next day, during the last hour of school, Mrs. Klingman's class and Ms. Freeman's class held a combined going-away party. Sebastian drank a cup of punch, ate a cookie, and spoke briefly with two boys who lived in his neighborhood. Stanley Beal stood a good head taller than Marcus Franks, and even Marcus was taller than Sebastian. The two said they were going to the same two-week summer camp and couldn't wait. Sebastian said he looked forward to his family's trip to Utah to see the national parks there. His father had said they might go to the Great Salt Lake, too. They all stood in silence for a time, munching on their cookies, until Sebastian said, "Maybe I'll see you later this summer."

"Sure," said Stanley. "We'll be around."

Sketchbook in hand, Sebastian selected a desk out of the way of his milling school mates. He alternated between focusing on his sketchbook and watching Ms. Freeman serve punch to the students bunched around the refreshment table. She smiled and laughed and talked while she handed out the punch. For this last day, she had worn blue jeans and a hot pink tee shirt with a pattern of silver sequins that spelled out "LOVE LIFE" across the front. He drew the scene. In it, her left hand was raised to push her hair back over her shoulder while the long, slender fingers of her right hand curled around a punch cup.

When the final bell rang, everyone scurried after backpacks and raced out the door. Sebastian, too, shouldered his backpack, but he moved slower than most exiting the building. He settled himself under the big oak tree near the bike rack. He watched a group of kids jostle each other as they clambered up the bus steps for their school year's last ride home. Others ran toward their parents' cars, calling back and forth to each other about their summer plans. Two fourth-grade girls giggled as they retrieved their matching pink bicycles from the rack and rode away side-by-side.

Sebastian pulled out his drawing pad and began slowly leafing through it. He frequently glanced toward the entrance to his classroom building. After thirty minutes or so, Ms. Freeman finally exited and walked toward the teachers' parking lot. He shoved the drawings back into his backpack and ran after her. When he was within a few paces of her he blurted, "Ms. Freeman."

She turned and flashed her wide white smile at him. "Sebastian," she said. "I thought you left without saying goodbye, and I really wanted to say goodbye."

"Yes, ma'am," he said. "Me too. I wanted to give you something." He swung his backpack off his shoulder, unzipped it, and reached in for his sketchbook.

"How sweet." She laid a hand on his shoulder. "I'll miss you, Sebastian." She bent at the waist, leaned in and kissed his cheek. He turned his head slowly, his lips nearing hers. She straightened. "But I know you'll have a great summer. And guess what? They told me this morning that I'll be hired for next year, so I'll see you then."

His shoulders slumped. "I'll be in middle school," he said. "I won't be here."

"I know. But it's just a few blocks away. I'll come see you. Or maybe you'll come see me."

"Yes, ma'am."

She smiled and patted his shoulder again. "Anyway, you'll have a great summer. Keep drawing, okay?"

"Okay," he said.

"And I, too, will have a great summer," she said. "My boyfriend just finished college and he got a job here in town."

"Boyfriend?"

She nodded and grinned broadly. "When he moves here, I'm pretty sure he's going to propose."

"Propose?"

"And," she said, "I want you to come to the wedding. I want you to draw pictures of it. Would you do that?"

Sebastian's face burned and his eyes stung, but he managed a nod. "Yes, ma'am."

"Terrific. It's a deal then." She extended her hand. He took it, gripped firmly as his father had taught him, and they shook. "Oh," she said, "what did you want to give me?"

He looked away from her, down into his backpack. "I'm sorry," he said. "I guess I left it at home."

"Well," she said smiling, "that means you'll have to come see me next fall so you can give it to me then."

"Yes, ma'am."

"Remember, Sebastian, you keep drawing. I want to see all your work next year."

"Yes, ma'am."

She turned and strolled toward the parking lot, slipped into the Carolla, and was gone. His face still burning, Sebastian walked toward the bicycle rack, but just before he reached it, he veered to the right and sat on the ground under the tree.

He slipped his backpack off and unzipped it. He pulled his sketchbook out and flipped the pages to the first drawing of Ms. Freeman. He carefully pulled it away from the pad's binding. Then he did the same with the second drawing, the third, and the fourth. He stacked the drawings together, folded them neatly in half and then in half again. He pinched the folds between his thumb and forefinger and slid the fingers across the creases, making them tighter. He stood up and walked to the large trash can near the bike rack. He pushed open its swinging lid just a crack and slipped the folded papers in and released them. Then he strode to his bike and pedaled away from elementary school for the last time.

II. The Tony Hawkins Stories

Just One of the Guys

Nell Crane turned twelve the first day of summer vacation 1966. I would turn twelve before the summer ended. Nell was a tomboy and my best friend from kindergarten through the summer of 1966. She played football, basketball, and baseball better than most of us boys. She could scramble up a rocky hillside, bait a hook, or trade punches with the best of us. On the school bus, she joined our belching contests and usually won. In sixth grade, she tried chewing tobacco with us; she chewed a bigger plug, spit farther, and threw up more than any of the rest of us. Nell was great. Nell had always been just one of the guys. But by that summer of 1966, guys had become more interested in gawking at girls' budding breasts than in fishing or chewing tobacco with them. They didn't gawk at Nell, but neither did they invite her fishing or slap her on the back and ask, "How's it hangin'?" For me, though, Nell was just Nell. A friend. A bud.

That summer Nell went to camp the day after her birthday and didn't appear again until three weeks later when she showed up at the park in Stanley Mincus's neighborhood. Seven of us boys sat Indian-style choosing sides for a game of football. Nell's bike kicked up a cloud of dust when she skidded to a stop in front of us.

"Can I play?" she asked. She dropped her bike on its side and plopped down next to me. She smelled like coconut.

We waved the dust out of our faces. "We're gonna play football," Mincus said.

"I like football." Nell pulled the ball from my hands. She tossed it up in a spiral, caught it, tossed it up again. Her arms were deeply tanned.

"Tackle," Matt Schroeder said as if that clearly excluded Nell.

"I like tackle." She tossed the ball to Schroeder. Caught off guard, he didn't get his hands up in time. The ball bounced off his chest and rolled out of reach. "Good catch," Nell said. Dappled sunlight through the pecan branches above us flecked her straight brown hair, not quite shoulder length.

"Shut up," Schroeder said. He got up to fetch the ball.

"We've already picked teams," said David Price. He looked at Nell and shrugged.

"Can't you count?" she asked. "They're uneven." Her hair fell across her right cheek. She pushed it back with one finger, tucked it behind her ear. It fell back across her face.

Schroeder had the ball by then and walked toward the open area where we played. Mincus stood up to follow. "It's just the guys today," he said. "Com on, y'all."

We all stood up. Nell brushed dirt off the seat of her pants, then looked at me. "I'm just one of the guys," she said.

"Don't be stupid," Price said over his shoulder.

Nell ignored him. She looked straight at me, cocked her head. "Well?" she said. Her eyebrows arched with the question and her lips formed a tentative smile. Her dark brown eyes reflected the speckles of sunlight filtering through the trees.

"My team's the short one," I said. "We rotate quarterbacking. You okay with that?"

The tentative smile broke into a full grin. "Thanks, Tony. You're the best." She slapped my shoulder and kept her hand there as we trotted toward the field.

The other guys accepted her grudgingly, but as the game intensified they forgot that she was supposed to be different. She was just another player. She was just one of the guys. We played for an hour before calling a time out and racing to a rusty old water faucet near the picnic tables. After a drink, we collapsed onto our backs in the shade of a pecan tree. We pulled our tee-shirts halfway up our stomachs so the slight breeze could better cool us. Price lifted a leg and farted. Schroeder lifted a leg and tried but failed. Nell laughed. Her taut brown stomach rose and fell rhythmically with her laughter.

Cooled and rested, none of us felt much like going back to the game. But since we had stopped with the score tied we agreed to play until the next touchdown. My team received the ball. It was Nell's turn to quarterback. She called a pass play with me as the receiver. After we broke our huddle and lined up, she stepped up beside me, draped her left arm across my shoulders, cupped her right hand to my ear, and whispered a last-minute change in the pass pattern. She leaned in close as she spoke, and her lips brushed my ear. They felt soft, her breath warm.

"Wait," I said when she pulled away. "What did you say?"

She scowled, grabbed my forearm, pulled me close and whispered again. A small scab crusted one knuckle of the hand that held my arm. I placed my forefinger on the scab, rubbed it gently. The unnaturally white ring of flesh around it contrasted with the tan of the rest of her finger. She pulled her hand away and I realized she had repeated the play change.

"Wait," I said sheepishly. "One more time?"

She grasped my head between her hands, shoved her face into mine. Our foreheads and noses touched. "What's wrong with you!" she scolded. "Pay attention." Her breath smelled Juicy Fruit sweet. She twisted my head sideways and whispered the play for a third time.

I ran the wrong pattern and couldn't get open. Nell dodged, scrambled, broke for the goal line and made the deciding touchdown. My team ran to congratulate her while the other guys argued amongst themselves about whose fault their loss was. When everybody finally headed for the water faucet, I hung back with Nell. "Great play," I said, too embarrassed to look her in the face.

"Yeah," she said, "no thanks to you."

I shrugged. "Sorry about that." Her sweaty tee-shirt clung to her. I realized for the first time that, like most of the other girls, she too had grown small breasts.

She cocked her head, smiled. "Well, you were smart enough to let me play. I guess I can forgive you for being otherwise stupid."

"You're so kind," I replied sarcastically. We grinned and high-fived. She was a good friend. I squeezed her hand to let her know. She squeezed back briefly but then pulled away and trotted off to taunt the losers.

We saw each other again two days later when her parents invited my family to dinner. The adults visited around the outdoor grill, drinking cocktails and watching the fat burgers cook. Her mother snapped photographs of everyone. Nell and I sat shoulder-to-shoulder in the yard, our backs against a huge oak tree, our bare legs stretched out in the cool grass. She smelled like coconut, just like the day of the football game. It must have been her shampoo. Our legs touched, her skin smooth and cool against mine. We made whistles from blades of St. Augustine cupped in our hands, then chewed on the grass blades and planned for a huge neighborhood game of Hide-and-Seek after dinner. Smoke from the grill, heavy with the scent of sizzling burgers, wafted past us. I felt starved.

After burgers and chips and homemade ice cream, we ventured into her neighborhood to roust out enough kids for the Hide-and-Seek marathon. By dusk, we wearied of the game, but Mary Boggus, who lived across the street from Nell, insisted on one more round so that she could be "IT." She covered her eyes and began counting loudly to fifty. Everyone scattered. Worn out, I simply stepped around the side of the house and hunkered behind the air conditioning unit. By the time Mary reached thirty, I realized what a stupid place I had chosen, too close to Mary and one of the first places she'd look. I crept to the corner of the house and peered through the dimming light. While Mary made her way from thirty-five to forty, I scanned the back yard for a better hiding place. At forty, I sprinted the length of the yard to a tarp-covered firewood pile in the far corner. At forty-five, I squeezed between the fence and wood pile and ducked under the tarp. At forty-eight, my forehead smacked someone else's.

"Get out!" Nell whispered intensely.

Mary hit fifty. "I'll get caught," I whispered back.

Nell pressed her forehead harder against mine, as if to push me out. "I don't care." Sweaty forehead to sweaty forehead, we strained against each other, panting for breath in that little pocket of heavy, dead air thick with odors of oil and sawdust from the tarp and the woodpile. Filtered through those heavy odors was the lighter one of Nell's Juicy Fruit breath.

I kissed her straight on the lips.

Her hands flashed to my chest and pushed me backwards. I squinted, gritted my teeth, prepared for the coming pain. But after an unbearably silent, breathless pause, she did not pound my face with her fists. Instead, she gathered folds of my tee-shirt into her fists, yanked me forward, and pressed her lips hard against mine. We exploded into a flurry of desperate, awkward kisses. My mouth filled with the taste of her Juicy Fruit. My nostrils frantically sucked for air and burned with the pungent oil and sawdust smells.

Somehow over the sounds of our own smacking and panting, we heard Mary's footsteps as she jogged toward the woodpile. Nell clutched my throat and squeezed with her strong fingers. "If you tell," she whispered, "I'll kill you." I tried to answer, but only a croak could gurgle past the spot where she squeezed my windpipe.

For several weeks, Nell and I avoided each other's company. Then my family went camping in Colorado. By the time we returned to Texas, I could pretend to forget the night of kissing. Three days after returning, I wheeled my bike into Nell's driveway, hoping that she, too, could pretend to forget.

She stood on a ladder painting the outer wall of a store room connected to their carport. I leaned my bike against the house, stuffed my hands in my pockets, and walked slowly toward the ladder.

"Hey, Nell."

She glanced over her shoulder. "Hey," she said and resumed painting. "When did you get back?"

"Couple days ago." I waited for some question about the trip, but she said nothing. I removed my right hand from its pocket and dabbed my forefinger in a freckle of paint on the ladder's second rung. It was an old drip, dry and smooth to the touch. "So," I said, "what're you doing?"

"Painting." Her tone clarified the stupidity of my question.

I looked up from the freckle of paint. She had outgrown the black shorts she wore. They fit tighter and shorter than anything she wore in public. "I'm headed to Mincus's park," I said. "You know, just to see if anybody's around." She rolled onto her toes to reach a high spot with her paint brush. "You want to go?" I asked.

"My dad's paying me," she said. "I better keep painting." The tight muscles of her long legs flexed as she stretched for that high spot.

"Okay." I shoved my hand back into my pocket. "See you later."

Before I reached my bike, she called, "Hey, Tony." She had descended the ladder and stood looking at me with her head cocked and that tentative smile on her face. "You really want me to go?"

"Yeah. Sure."

She grinned. "I gotta change first." With a downward glance she indicated her paint-speckled tee-shirt and shorts. The red shirt fit as tightly as the shorts, and I could tell she wore nothing underneath. A small inverted dimple dotted the fabric on either side of her chest. Heat prickled my face. "Come on," she said. "You can have a Dr Pepper while you wait." Inside, she waved toward the kitchen. "You know where they are. Get me one, too."

"Where's your mom?" I called as she disappeared around the hallway corner.

"Shopping," she hollered back.

I pulled two bottles of Dr Pepper from the bottom shelf of their refrigerator, then found the opener in its usual drawer. The bottles hissed at me when I popped their caps off. The smooth glass bottles felt cold against my palms.

By the time I entered her room, Nell had already changed shorts. She held a fresh tee-shirt in one hand, accepted with the other the Dr Pepper I offered. "Thanks." She drained half of the bottle in one gulp. She belched, then said, "I'm gonna wash up a little and change shirts." In the bathroom, she pushed the door to, but not quite closed.

An image of her red tee-shirt and those two inverted dimples flashed through my mind. My face prickled. I leaned against the bathroom door jamb, breathed in the coconut scent seeping through the sliver of open space. "Can I come in?" I asked.

The sound of running tap water muffled her voice. "No way!"

Though she couldn't see me, I shrugged. "Why not?"

"Don't be stupid, Tony."

I closed my eyes, sucked in that coconut smell. "No, really," I said. "I thought you were just one of the guys."

"I am." The water stopped running. A towel rack squeaked. "But this is different."

"How come?"

"Well . . . ." She hesitated, then started again. "Well, you don't kiss the other guys, do you?"

Those pinpricks of heat poked at face more insistently. "No. Of course not."

"Okay then."

76

I swigged my Dr Pepper. The cold bubbles burned my throat. "But I've seen them change shirts lots of times."

An aerosol can spoke first: two quick hisses of spray deodorant. Nell spoke second: "Well you won't see me."

I took another swig of Dr Pepper. "Okay," I said. "I guess you're not just one of the guys after all." I stepped away from the door, set my bottle on her dresser. Numerous small picture frames stood on the dresser, at least half of them displaying photographs of Nell and me. There we were, kindergartners, muddy from head to toe, grinning like idiots as we stomped through a puddle. There we were, maybe seven or eight, standing by a swimming pool and flexing our biceps. There we were, just a summer ago, squatting on the banks of the Guadalupe with long cane poles in our hands. There we were, a few short weeks ago, leaning shoulder-to-shoulder against that huge oak tree, blowing into cupped hands to make blades of St. Augustine sing.

"I am," Nell said, her voice quiet, her tone sad. I turned toward the opened bathroom door. "I am just one of the guys." She faced me. The heels of her palms rested on the bathroom counter, her fingers curled underneath it. She stared down at the tee-shirts, the tight red one and the fresh one lying at her feet. Her hair fell forward, hid her face entirely.

My stomach suddenly felt as icy as that Dr Pepper bottle, but my face felt on fire. My gaze remained fixed on Nell's bare chest. My legs moved me shakily into the bathroom. After what must have been a minute or more, my hand trembled toward her. She winced when my palm, still cold from the bottle, pressed against her bare skin. A car door slammed.

"My mother!" Nell shoved me into the bedroom and slammed the bathroom door before I could register what we'd heard. But when it registered, I moved quickly to slip out the back door before Mrs. Crane stepped through the front door.

I circled the house to the driveway. I fetched Nell's basketball from the carport and stepped off ten feet from the goal. My first shot went wide, my second fell short, my third both wide and short. I paced out to the street, counting my steps, then paced back to my bike. I mounted the bike and rode circles in the driveway. When Nell stepped out the door, I stopped.

"You ready?" I asked.

She walked toward the end of the driveway, and I followed. Near the street, she turned and cocked her head, but not even a tentative smile appeared. "It was a trick, wasn't it, Tony?"

"What was a trick?" I studied the tiny mole above her eyebrow.

"What you said. You know, about me being just one of the guys."

"No." I leaned over to flick a pebble from the tread of my bike tire. "I mean. . . well . . . I don't know. Listen, Nell, I'm sorry."

"Me too," she said and turned to face the road. "You better go."

"You're not coming?" I asked. She shook her head. "Maybe next time, huh?"

"Yeah," she said. "Maybe."

I peddled out of the driveway and coasted down the short hill leading away from their house. At the bottom, I glanced over my shoulder to wave, but Nell had already turned her back. I focused on the flat stretch of road ahead and peddled hard.

Seeing Gina

Mike Salley, my best friend and closest neighbor, had seen Gina Veck's titties, and I wanted my turn. I found out one sunny October Saturday morning when I helped him dig weeds out of the huge yard his dad insisted on keeping perfectly manicured. Finished, we traipsed down to the little creek that crossed his property and settled under a sycamore to sneak a smoke. Mike pulled the crumpled pack out of his back pocket, dug a cigarette out, and passed the pack to me. He lit the cigarette, flattened from being hidden under his mattress, and exhaled the smoke in a slow, thin stream between pursed lips. As he handed the lighter to me he said, "I saw Gina Veck's titties yesterday."

Mike was the best I knew at starting and maintaining a good bullshit. My hand hung in the air near the lighter he offered while I studied his face for signs that's what he was up to: raised eyebrows, that half smile that twitched at the corners. But they weren't there. Instead, he grinned like the proverbial possum eating persimmons.

"You gonna take this lighter?" he asked, and I did.

I flicked open the Zippo and lit up. I leaned back against the sycamore, propped my elbows on my knees. "You gotta be shitting me."

"Hand to God, T.H. She even let me touch them."

"So, tell me. Tell me, man."

We were fifteen, and despite our tragically limited first-hand experience titties were a favorite subject of every guy in school with the possible exception of Bruce Franklin who wore pink shirts and drew fashion designs in art class. And now Mike, the lucky bastard, had finally seen some. Granted, they were just Gina Veck's, but they still counted.

Gina hardly had titties, not to speak of. In fact, she had no shape at all. Though tall, she was not leggy. Though slender, she was not shapely.

79

Her height derived from an unusually long torso, the waist of which was exactly the same width as her bony hips. No one gave her a second look, usually not even a first, partly because of her shape, partly because of her reputation. She was known as a prude. Most of the girls our age had begun dating older boys, boys with cars. Grapevine said Gina had, to everyone's surprise, been asked out once or twice but had said her parents wouldn't allow it. Nobody believed her. Her mother was ordinarily too drunk to care, her father too busy boffing other men's wives.

Mike and I lived about three miles outside the city limits in a sparsely populated Texas Hill Country neighborhood. His folks owned fifty-seven acres. I lived on twenty-two acres across the county road from him. Gina's family had moved to a house about half a mile from us, closer to the main road, when we were in fifth grade. For a time, folks in the area invited them to get-togethers, and us kids always had fun. Though neither of us would admit it, Mike and I both thought Gina was cute, and we did what fifth-graders do to vie for her attention; we told stupid jokes, made stupid faces, and took stupid prat falls just to hear her laugh because laughing meant she liked us. But soon everything changed. Her mother, it turned out, was a foul-mouthed sloppy drunk, her dad a nasty lech who copped not-so-subtle feels from all the other women every chance he got. Within a few months, they disappeared from neighborhood gatherings, shunned by all the adults who talked about them when they didn't know we were listening. Mike and I would occasionally see Gina walking Gunther, her German Shepard, and visit with her if we couldn't find a way to avoid it, but, embarrassed, we excused ourselves as soon as possible.

But now, four years later, she'd shown her titties to Mike—more than shown, apparently, and I wanted to know all about it. I figured any girl who'd show her titties to one guy would show them to another, and the more I knew the better my chances of getting in on the action.

Mike flipped his cigarette butt into the little stream that gurgled a few feet away from the sycamore and began his tale. Since school started, he said, Gina and Gunther had been popping up more often than usual wherever he happened to be—down by the creek, back at the big tank his dad kept stocked with bass and catfish, at his house where he might be doing yard work or just kicking around waiting for me to show up. We spent most of our free time together, mostly outdoors, but Gina generally appeared before I arrived or after I had left, Mike explained. At first, their exchanges followed the typical pattern: "Hey, Mike," she'd say.

"Hey, Gina. What's up?"

"Nothing. Walking Gunther. You?"

"Nothing. Catching frogs."

"Well, see you later."

"Yeah, see you later."

That was the usual extent of conversations. But lately she'd been lingering, asking him about school, about his weekend plans, about frogs. Basically, about anything that extended their time together. Her behavior baffled him, and he did everything he could to cut that time as short as possible. Then, on the day before we grubbed weeds, when he had made some excuse and turned to leave her, she had grabbed his elbow. When he turned back, she studied his face and then said, "Do you like me?"

Anyone would be hard-pressed to say they liked Gina Veck. But it's tough to tell a girl whose face is a few inches from yours that you don't care about her one way or the other. So Mike said, "Yeah. Sure. I guess."

And she kissed him square on the lips. Shocked by the unexpected move, he flinched, pulled back, and then immediately regretted the instinctive action. Her lips were thin, he said, and cold, but they felt soft and eager, and making out was making out, even if it were with Gina Veck. She blushed, and he blushed. She apologized and he apologized. They both stood looking at their feet until she finally said, "Do you want to see me?"

Seeing a girl meant dating her, and while he thought that seeing Gina might be better than seeing no one, he didn't especially want to be seen *with* her. "I don't know," he said. "I mean, I can't drive. I don't know how."

"No," she said. "I mean see me."

He thought maybe she meant they could meet like this again, which wouldn't be so bad. No one would know, but he could get in some good make-out practice. "You mean, like, tomorrow or something?" He finally brought himself to look at her, but she still looked at the ground.

"No," she said. "I mean, like, right now." She tugged at Gunther's leash and led the dog a few paces away, deeper into the oak grove bordering the creek. She wrapped his leash around a small trunk and peeled her faded red tee shirt off. She tossed the shirt over near Gunther

81

and faced Mike. She wore no bra. "See?" she said. Mike gaped from his spot near the creek. Gunther nosed the tee-shirt. "You can touch, too, if you like."

He liked.

"Shit, Mike," I said. "Gina Veck's titties!"

"And," he grinned, "she said we could do it again."

"Shit, Mike!"

"They're not big, you know" he said. "But they're . . . I don't know . . . they're . . . you know, they're . . . nice."

I needed no convincing. They might have been small. They might have belonged to Gina Veck. But they were still honest-to-goodness titties available for viewing, and I was more than a willing viewer. "Shit, Mike," I said.

During the week after he reported his good fortune, I kept a watchful eye on the neighborhood every afternoon. All I had to do was spot Gina walking Gunther before she found Mike and I'd have some good fortune of my own to report. My chance arrived on Friday. Mike had a dentist appointment after school, and I wandered the creek bed on my property but hung close enough to the county road to see Gina if she happened by. And she did, in fact, happen by. When she reached the low-water crossing where the creek flowed under the road through a huge concrete drain pipe, she waded through the tall weeds lining the road and climbed the fence onto Mike's place. Once over the fence, she lifted the bottom wires so that Gunther could join her. She strolled slowly downstream, allowing Gunther to stop and sniff at whatever pleased him. Eventually, they disappeared around a bend in the creek. That's when I began following the route she had taken.

I acted surprised when I rounded that bend and saw her about thirty feet downstream. "Hey, Gina," I said as casually as possible. My palms dampened in anticipation.

"Hey, Tony."

"What's up?" I asked, walking oh-so casually closer.

"Nothing. Walking Gunther." She looked at the dog, not at me. "You?"

"Nothing. Catching frogs."

It was one of those wonderfully warm, sunny October afternoons.

She wore cut-offs and what I assumed was the same faded red tee-shirt Mike had watched her drop by Gunther's nose. The breeze blew her hair across her face but she made no move to push it back. In the ensuing silence I stared at her shirt, straining to determine whether she wore a bra. She folded her arms across her chest. She'd nailed me. Feeling the warmth spread through my face, I feigned sudden interest in a rock near my foot. I pushed at it with the toe of my tennis shoe. I leaned forward, turned it over with my hand. I studied it long and hard, picked it up, hefted it, then finally let it drop.

"Thought it was a fossil," I said when I felt the blush pass.

"Was it?" she asked, totally deadpan.

"No." I kept my eyes off her chest, focused from the neck up.

She watched Gunther paw at something in the shallow water, and after a few more seconds of awkward silence, she said, "Well, see you later." She tightened the slack in Gunther's leash to urge him away from the water. I saw my chances trickling away downstream.

Desperate, I blurted, "Yeah, I'd like that."

She looked up from Gunther to me. "Like what?"

We made eye contact and I felt the warmth in my face again. I shoved my hands in my pockets and shrugged. "I don't know. I mean, you know, to see you later." Later, in truth, was not an option I preferred, so I added lamely, "Or, you know, whenever."

Embarrassed by the blush, I had averted my eyes. I stared off into the oak grove, imagined her saying, *How about right now*. She had said it to Mike, so she'd surely say it to me as well, would say it and then step into the shadows of those trees, peel off that faded shirt, beckon me to join her, to touch, to fondle, to know the sweet softness I imagined, yearned for, ached for.

But she said nothing. Disappointed, I stole a glance and was surprised at how small she seemed. I flashed on her first few months in the neighborhood, on those gatherings her family attended. I remembered how happily she played and joked and laughed with Mike and me and how quickly she curled inside herself when her mother started spewing vulgarities or fell face down in the dirt or in someone's lap. That's what I saw there by the creek. Her shoulders drooped, her neck curved forward, her face down, her arms crossed and clutched her midsection. Gunther apparently noticed, too. He pressed his side against her legs, licked her knees, whined a little. She dropped a hand to his head, scratched listlessly. Without looking up, she said, "He told you, didn't he?" Her voice had changed, too, almost a whisper, a hoarse, feeble whisper like my grandmother's.

My tongue felt numb, my head empty. "Listen, Gina," was all I managed before pausing to search for the next words.

"It wasn't his to tell," she said. When she looked up, I saw that she was crying. If it weren't for their source, the tear streaks might have been pretty because they highlighted her clear complexion and emphasized the smooth curve of her cheekbones. Her tears shimmered in the late afternoon sunlight and intensified the soft green shade of her eyes. She hugged herself and shivered. "It wasn't his," she said. "Don't you see?"

"Yeah," I said, but I didn't see. Not exactly, anyway. "Listen, Gina," I tried again but again got no further.

She turned without tightening Gunther's leash, but he followed immediately just the same. "See you, Tony," she said over her shoulder as she shuffled into the oaks.

"Yeah," I said. "See you, Gina." I watched until the trees swallowed her out of sight, then still stood squinting through the branches for a couple of minutes, maybe more.

Back on the county road, I trudged up the short hill toward my driveway. My legs felt heavy, my throat constricted. I wondered if I was catching my first fall cold. I stepped aside for the car I heard approaching from behind. It pulled up beside me and stopped. Mike stepped out from the passenger side and slammed the door, and his mother drove on.

"Clean teeth?" I asked.

"Clean teeth," he chuckled. "No cavities. Where you been?"

"Just walking."

"Got smokes?"

I shook my head.

"Let's go grab mine," he said.

"I don't feel so good, Mike. I think I'll just go home."

"Come on, T.H.," he cajoled. "I've been trapped in the damned dentist chair. I need a smoke."

"Maybe later."

He sighed. "Okay, man. Better for me to be alone anyway. I might see Gina."

"Yeah, you might." My throat tightened more, and I focused on moving my leaden legs.

"Shit, Tony," Mike said. "What the hell's wrong with you?"

"Told you, I'm sick." After a couple more steps, I paused, turned back. Mike had already jumped into the weedy ditch and begun struggling up the opposite side toward his fence. "Hey, Mike," I called.

He turned only after topping the ditch. "What?"

"I really do hope you see her," I said. "I hope you really do *see* Gina." But I knew he never would.

Brenda with Skin

When summer began between my junior and senior year in high school, my life felt complicated. Then Mrs. Grogan stripped naked in front of me and complicated it even more.

It started with Carol Mayfield. Our freshman year, Carol, who had probably been beautiful from the day she was born, blossomed in all the right places. All the girls wanted to be her friends. All the boys just wanted her. If rumor had it right, she wanted them, too, and any guy old enough to take her on a car date received a gift from her the likes of which he'd never received before. Despite what I liked to believe about myself, I was a little naive about and more than a little awkward around girls. Even when I got my license, I didn't dare ask her out. By early in our junior year she settled in with one guy, David Taylor, and by the end of that year everybody said they'd probably get married someday.

But during the last few weeks of the school year, Carol had been touching me more than usual and flashing me glimpses of her lovely flesh. She doled those treats out daily: a short skirt that rode up too high when she sat in the desk across from me in English, or a split skirt that fell open too far when she slipped into that desk, or a loose blouse that gapped at the top when she dropped a pen and leaned down in front of me to pick it up, or a hand gently touching my shoulder or elbow as we spoke in the hallway, or even a brush of boob against my arm as we walked toward class.

On the last day of school she told me that her family was vacationing the first two weeks of June. I observed that David Taylor would surely miss her. She shrugged, then said that he'd be gone the next two weeks after that. "Then," she said, "I'll just be around." She cupped her palm around my elbow. "You know, just hanging out. Looking for something to

87

do."

That seemed like a pretty clear invitation to me. But David Taylor complicated matters. He was a decent guy, and he was nuts about Carol. When I thought about him I felt bad about what I hoped might happen with her during his absence. So I tried not to think about him and set about finding a job so I could afford the kind of date Carol deserved for the kind of treat she would surely bestow on me. Still, David kept popping into my head. It was complicated.

And then Mrs. Grogan stripped naked in front of me.

My family lived outside the city limits of a small Texas Hill Country town. Our house sat off a winding gravel road about half a mile from the main road. Gerald Grogan and his wife, Brenda, lived about a half mile farther down the winding gravel road. He made an average living selling insurance from a little rented office in town. Childless themselves, they had always been great to the few of us kids who lived in the area, and they were devoted and generous friends to our parents as well.

Their house sat on ten or twelve beautiful hill country acres, and Mr. Grogan hired me to do odd jobs that his work left him little time to do himself. My first task was to clear rocks from an area that sloped from their house down to a small stream that passed through their property. The slope was wild with tall grass and low-growing shrubs, and he wanted me to clear all the rocks and cut out the shrubs so he could mow the slope and have a clear view of the stream from his back patio.

My first day on the job, I woke early, restless with thoughts of Carol and, unfortunately, David. To work off my nervous energy, I walked rather than drove back to the Grogans' place. About half way, Mr. Grogan passed on his way to work. He waved. I waved back, then listened to the crunch of gravel beneath his tires as it faded farther away. Before long, though, I heard that crunch again, vague at first but progressively louder, progressively closer. The car that passed was unmistakable. Mr. Veck, another neighbor in our sparsely populated neighborhood, owned the only gold Cadillac anywhere in the county. That's why his behavior seemed so odd. He wore sunglasses and a cap pulled low over his face, as if to disguise himself, and when he passed he slid down in his seat so that his head was barely visible. As if I wouldn't recognize his car, I thought. Odd. Very odd.

When I arrived at the Grogans', his car sat in the driveway. Perhaps an hour later, as I dumped my fourth or fifth wheel barrow full of rocks into a little gulley Mr. Grogan had specified, Mr. Veck's gold Cadillac eased out of the driveway. Again, he wore the sunglasses and cap and slumped in his seat. I shook my head and rolled the wheel barrow back to my spot on the rocky slope. Mrs. Grogan, wearing a knee-length silky robe, called to me from the back porch. When I reached the porch, raised about a foot higher than the ground because of the sloped land, I tilted my head back to look up at her. She was in her late thirties or early forties but still had the looks of a much younger woman. The other few boys in the neighborhood and I had often talked about her looks after some neighborhood gathering to which she had worn a shorter skirt than the other women or a V-neck blouse that revealed so much lovely cleavage.

The sun, just barely above the rooftop, silhouetted her and made a sort of halo around her strawberry-blond hair, combed, perhaps, with her fingers but still tousled. Sexy, I thought. Very sexy. She smiled and asked how the work was going. I said fine. She nodded, still smiling, and ran fingers through her hair.

"We were planning a surprise," she said and tilted her head in the direction Mr. Veck's car had disappeared. "A party for Gerald."

"Oh," I said, staring, I fear, at her breasts rather than her face.

"A surprise," she emphasized. "You'll help keep it a secret, won't you?"

"Yes, mam," I said. I avoided eye contact.

She laid her palm against my cheek, the fingers long and soft and warm. "Thanks. You're a fine young man." I blushed and turned back toward my work.

I filled the wheelbarrow again and straightened, hands on hips, to catch my breath. I looked up the incline toward the house. The curtains of a plate glass window at one end of the house were open, and Mrs. Grogan stood at the foot of a bed slipping that robe off her shoulders. It fell to the floor, and she proceeded to peel a skimpy night gown off over her head. Although she faced away from me, the sight of all that woman flesh and that beautifully rounded ass virtually stopped my heart and my breath. And then, when she turned toward the window, interlaced her fingers behind her neck, and stretched, my bones went liquid and I barely managed to stay on my feet. I stood frozen in that spot, staring until she finished her stretch and disappeared off to the right, where I assumed the bathroom was.

When I finally forced myself back to rock gathering, I couldn't stop replaying my view of her, and then my imagination followed her into the shower. I could see her hair, wet and slicked back, rivulets of water running down her back and rolling gracefully over that still-tight butt, little glistening drops hanging momentarily on her nipples before dripping onto her flat stomach and then gathering in those lovely, mysterious curly hairs below, or running past the hair and down those long, slender legs.

I shook those images out of my head as best I could and tried to focus on rock gathering. But I still kept wondering: had she simply forgotten to pull the curtains closed; had she provided me that little gift as a bribe, a way to keep me quiet about her meeting with Mr. Veck; or had she shown me what I could have if I only asked?

Carol and David. And now Mrs. Grogan and Mr. Grogan and Mr. Veck. My life felt more complicated by the minute.

To distract myself, I drove to town that evening to see who might be around. People often gathered at the Dairy Queen early in the evening until formulating a better plan or heading off to something already planned, so that's where I started. The place was pretty empty, so I ordered a burger and waited to see who might show. David Taylor walked through the door first. I waved to him, hoping he was meeting others and wouldn't stop to chat. No such luck. He grabbed a burger and headed straight to my booth. He had nothing much to do, he said, with Carol out of town. He sure did miss her, he said. It would be a long June without her; his family would leave for two weeks a day before her family returned. He sure loved her, he said, and had been thinking a lot about the future, had been seriously thinking about marrying her right after graduation next May. He'd have to postpone college, but he said she was worth it.

I felt sorry for the guy. There he was pining for his absent girlfriend, thinking about marriage, with no clue what she'd been up to with me the last few weeks, no clue that he sat there confiding in the guy she wanted to see while he was out of town. Just as Mr. Grogan had no clue Mr. Veck had paid a visit, or that his wife had stripped in full view of the boy who worked for him. Maybe I wouldn't call Carol after all. It didn't seem right. Or maybe I should just tell David. But that didn't seem right either. It would devastate him and probably ruin my chances with her. So all I said was, "Marriage. Wow. That's big."

The next morning, I walked to work again, saw Mr. Grogan and waved, listened to his tires crunch gravel, but, to my great relief, did not later hear the approach of other tires. Also to my great relief, the Grogans' bedroom curtains were fully closed. Mrs. Grogan never came out that day. I worked myself harder than I'd worked in my life, hoping to forget my complications. The rest of the week followed the same pattern: walk to work, wave to Mr. Grogan, check the window for a naked Mrs. Grogan, and then work myself to exhaustion. Mrs. Grogan might never strip for me again, but Carol's return grew closer every day, and I was certain that she could satisfy the cravings that her earlier actions and Mrs. Grogan's lovely flesh had intensified in me.

In the evenings, I'd go out. My parents wondered why I'd had no date so far and why I didn't stay home occasionally. I made up something about girls being out of town and about needing to get out after a hard day's work. They had always liked evenings when I stayed in, visited with them, maybe watched a little tv or played some cards. We got along fine, and I enjoyed those evenings as well, but that week I simply couldn't sit still. I'd head to town looking for something, anything to keep me occupied. And I'd always run into David Taylor somewhere. It made sense, I suppose. He was antsy, knocking around lonely, waiting for the day he could see Carol again. And I, too, was antsy, seeking distraction, waiting for the day I could see Carol again. In a town the size of ours, when you're looking to kill time, there are only so many places to kill it. So of course we would run into each other. I tried to steer conversation away from Carol and for the most part succeeded. And as soon as possible without seeming rude, I'd exit, making some excuse about somewhere I had to be.

On Monday morning, Mr. Veck returned. As before, he stayed about an hour, then drove off scrunched low in his seat. Before long, Mrs. Grogan opened the curtains and performed her nudie show. She stretched just as she had before, but she did not then head for the bathroom. Instead she went slowly about the business of making the bed, gathering up yesterday's clothes for the hamper, replacing a book on a small set of shelves near the bed. Several times she stopped to stretch, slowly, gracefully, beautifully. Finally she walked out of sight into the bathroom.

Maybe an hour after that she appeared on the patio and called to me. She wore a low cut red and white sun dress, it's hem about three or four inches above her knees. She had pulled her clean shimmering hair into a pony tail, and she smelled like roses or some other equally sweet bouquet.

"More party planning." She smiled down at me. I nodded. "You look exhausted," she said. "It's so hot today. Come up here. Come in and let me get you some ice water."

"Oh, no, mam. Thank you, but I'm fine."

"Nonsense," she said. She leaned from the edge of the patio to place a hand on my shoulder and pull me closer. "First of all, you get up here and come have some water. And second, don't call me mam." She grinned and laid that soft hand against my cheek. "I'm Brenda. You call me Brenda."

"Yes, mam," I said, oblivious to everything but the warmth of her hand on my cheek.

"Not mam," she reminded me. "Brenda."

"Yes, mam." I shook my head, blushed. "I mean Brenda." I stepped up onto the porch. She linked her arm around mine and led me through a side door into the kitchen. She pointed to a small table, and I sat. She filled a tall glass with ice, then with water, and set it in front of me. I drank, gulped really, draining nearly all of the water.

Standing across the table from me, she chuckled. "I knew you had to be thirsty." She bent at the waist, placed her palms on the table top. "Are you cooling down now?"

My view down the low-cut neckline of that sun dress made cooling down impossible, but I managed to nod. "Yes. Thank you."

She returned to the sink with the glass and began filling it again. I looked around the kitchen so as not to keep staring at her. A couple of pans leaned upside down in the dish drain, their handles pointing toward a wicker basket filled with apples and bananas. A coffee maker sat by the stove, the carafe that still contained a little cold coffee placed next to it. On the other side of the stove were some floor-to-ceiling cabinets and then the entrance to a laundry room. The laundry room was dim, but I could still make out a framed picture hanging on the wall above the dryer.

Mrs. Grogan set my water on the table. "You like that drawing?" she asked. She glided across the floor and flicked on a light in the laundry room. The frame contained a black-and-white drawing of a woman without hair or skin. It fascinated me, but repulsed me a little, too. "That's me," Mrs. Grogan said.

I looked at her and then back at the drawing. I'd seen such drawings, usually in color, in my biology textbook. This one appeared just as intricate and detailed. The shading highlighted the smooth curve of muscle and tendon and little pockets of fat.

Mrs. Grogan walked back to the table and sat in an end chair. "Not exactly the sort of thing you hang in the living room," she said. "But I like it, so I hung it where only I would have to look at it."

"It seems accurate," I said, unsure how else to respond.

"A boy from middle school used me as a model when I was in high school," she explained. "I didn't even know it. But he showed the drawings around. A friend of mine who had a brother in middle school got hold of that one and gave it to me." Her elbow on the table, she leaned her cheek on her palm and gazed at the drawing. "It fascinates me. I call it 'Brenda without Skin.' Do you like it?"

"Yes." I sipped my water.

She laughed. "You're very polite. But you're a teenage boy. I imagine you'd be far more interested in 'Brenda with Skin' than 'Brenda without Skin.'"

"Yes, mam," I blurted, then, realizing my mistake, quickly said, "I mean, no, mam." I pushed my chair back and stood up. "I better get back to work."

She laughed again. She, too, stood up, then moved next to me and put her arm around my shoulders as I stepped toward the door. "Listen," she said, "you don't have to work so hard. Come visit with me again, will you?"

I opened the door. "Yes, mam."

"Brenda," she said.

"Yes," I said. "Brenda."

She tightened the pressure of her arm on my shoulders. "Some morning, before you start work, come in and have coffee with me, or one of my sweet rolls."

"Okay." I eased out of her grasp. "Thanks for the water." I went back to work.

Mrs. Grogan's naked antics, the touch of her hand on my cheek or her arm around my shoulders, and, especially, her invitation to have one of her sweet rolls seemed as definite—more definite, even—than Carol's observation that she'd be alone looking for something to do. My concentration was so wrecked that I missed the wheelbarrow with several rocks I tried to toss into it and once crushed a finger between two rocks.

On my walk home that afternoon, I re-visualized that drawing of Brenda without skin, the muscles and tendons, imagined the perfect ways in which they tightened and slackened as she so gracefully stretched, fully in her skin, in front of that plate glass window. I was fairly certain that Mr. Veck knew exactly what her muscles could do for him as they lay in bed together, and I imagined what it would be like for me to lie with her skin-to-skin. I had no business, I knew, daydreaming about an adult, married woman. So I turned my thoughts to Carol and her lovely muscles, though in truth, as long as she had David Taylor I had no business thinking of her either.

That night, hoping to avoid David, I skipped the usual hang-outs, choosing instead to ease along winding back roads, thinking and thinking and thinking. Somewhere out on River Road, my front right tire picked up a nail, and my spare was flat. I locked the car and began my hike to town but had gotten no more than thirty or forty yards before a car approached from behind and pulled to stop as it came alongside me. None other than David Taylor stuck his head out the window. Having found no one to kill time with, he'd had about the same idea I'd had. He'd been meandering the back roads, just thinking, he said. We loaded my spare into his trunk, aired it up in town, and returned to my car. Despite my protests, he stayed to help me change the tire. Carol would be home on Friday, and I needed some time with her more than ever. But this guy, this really nice steady boyfriend of hers, wasn't making it easy. Unwitting as his actions had been, he was torturing me, complicating everything, tying my life in knots as if Mrs. Grogan hadn't done a good enough job of that already.

Every day for the rest of the week, I thought about Mrs. Grogan's invitation, and I thought about Carol's return on Friday. I likely didn't have the guts to knock on the Grogans' door pretending to want breakfast.

But worked up as I was, I'd definitely call Carol, David Taylor be damned.

So call her I did. The results were different than I expected. David's parents had postponed their departure a couple of days. They'd be leaving Sunday. "I'll be with him tonight," she said, "and tomorrow night."

"Oh."

"But listen, I'm glad you called. Really glad." She paused as if for a response, but I had none. After a brief silence, she said, "Call me again, okay? Sunday night, maybe."

"Okay," I managed. "Sunday night."

After the past two weeks, two more days should have seemed like nothing. Instead, they seemed to stretch like eternity before me. And so I spent a sleepless night working up the courage to knock on Mrs. Grogan's —Brenda's—door and ask for one of her sweet rolls in the morning.

I walked. I waved to Mr. Grogan as he headed for work. And I told myself I couldn't go through with it. But the plans I had made overnight carried my feet forward, straight to her door. I knocked. I waited maybe fifteen seconds. I knocked again. Waited again. She was probably still sleeping. I turned away, disappointment and relief flooding me simultaneously. The door opened.

"Good morning," she said.

She stood on the threshhold, one hand on the door knob, the other on the opposite jamb. My breath caught in my throat. She wore a silky peach colored nightgown that revealed perfect impressions of her nipples and didn't even reach mid-thigh. Clearly, though, she hadn't been sleeping. Her hair, as silky as the night gown, fell neatly brushed over her bare shoulders. She smelled, again, of roses. I was drowning in that smell, and lost in the sight of all her softness.

"I wanted," I said but then trailed off, thinking I sounded too demanding. "I mean, I was wondering . . . thinking . . . about your sweet rolls."

I suppose I expected her lovely smile, but instead she frowned. "Oh, sweetie, I'm sorry, but I have plans."

I was an idiot. Of course she had plans. She would always have plans. Her invitation had been simple politeness, like all invitations that specified not *a time* but that vague *sometime*. My cheeks burned.

I looked away from her, down at my shoes. "Okay," I managed.

"I'm sorry to have bothered you."

"No," she said, and her hands clutched either side of my face. "No, no, you didn't bother me." She tilted my head until my eyes met hers. Then her hands dropped from my face and clutched my hands. She squeezed them reassuringly. "I wanted you to come. I still do. Promise me. Promise you'll come another time." Words failed me, so I just nodded and stumbled away toward the tool shed.

By then I had cleared most of the rocks and had started in on the bushes. I fumbled in the shed for some long-handled clippers and a hatchet. Those innuendos, I wondered, was she aware of them? Were they intentional? And is *another time* any more definite than *sometime*? I attacked those bushes with a vengeance, clipping swiftly through the small stalks and hacking the thicker ones furiously with the hatchet. When Mr. Veck arrived, my attacks struck more viciously. But when Mr. Grogan arrived, I froze. I glanced up at the bedroom window, wondered if I had time to warn them, wondered if I even should. Soon, I heard a loud voice, Mr. Grogan's, I assumed, and a moment later, Mr. Veck's. I wasn't sure, but I thought I also heard crying. That would surely be Mrs. Grogan.

When the room fell quiet, I thought it best to take my tools back to the shed and disappear. The driveway was in clear view of the shed. By the time I threw the tools in and closed the door, Mr. Veck slumped into view, naked as Mrs. Grogan had been in front of the plate glass window. Mr. Grogan walked behind him, a shotgun in his hands, its barrel just inches from Mr. Veck's back. Mr. Veck begged for his clothes, but Mr. Grogan shoved the gun barrel against his back and pushed him toward his car. After the car roared out of the driveway, Mr. Grogan stood watching the dust cloud it left behind. His arms hung limp at his sides. He dropped the shotgun and then crumpled to the ground himself, legs crossed beneath him. He pushed his face into his upraised hands and wept—sobbed, really —like I had never heard a man sob in my life. I wanted to do something, to say something that would help. But I knew nothing would help. To avoid the driveway I walked down the slope to the creek, where I angled toward the fence line. I rolled under the barbed wire and scrambled up onto the gravel road.

My mother wondered why I came home so early. I said Mr. Grogan had changed his mind, didn't need my help after all. She asked if anything was wrong. I said no.

Sunday morning I slept late and then spent the afternoon helping my dad replace some rotted house siding. We tried conversation, but he could tell my mind was elsewhere and didn't pry, speaking only to provide instructions about the work at hand. Later that afternoon, I sat outside alone, staring into a thick copse of oaks behind our house. I imagined Carol Mayfield sitting at her house, maybe watching tv, waiting for me to call. I imagined David Taylor, on vacation with his family, not enjoying it much, wishing he were back home with Carol. I imagined Mrs. Grogan naked, imagined all her beautiful skin and the muscles beneath her skin. I imagined the ruckus at Mr. Veck's house when he came home naked. And I imagined Mr. Grogan sitting in his driveway sobbing.

Inside, I pulled the phone book from its drawer. I turned to Carol Taylor's number, even though I had committed it to memory two weeks before. I stared at that number for a long time, then closed the book and slipped it back into the drawer. Not tonight, I thought. Maybe sometime. But not tonight.

Stardust

This is a story about a girl I loved. Or perhaps a girl I daydreamed about loving. Or maybe just a girl I daydreamed about. Who knows?

Her name was Linda Starkey, and she was the cousin of one my best friends since grade school, Stanley Mincus. She was four years older and so paid little attention to us but, unlike lots of older kids, she always had a pleasant word, a kind word to say when her attention happened to drift our way. She never spoke a mean word to us or to anyone that I ever knew of.

Her father built a highly successful real estate career in the Texas hill country, and by 1962, when Linda was twelve, he bought a palatial house with a detached game room and a swimming pool. We were always welcome there, according to Linda, though I'm not sure her dad approved. He didn't seem to like kids much, or else he was basically unaware of them and irritated by reminders of their existence. Who knows? He was ex-military and maintained a strong sense of order. Around the game room and pool he had posted a number of neatly-penned lists of rules. But he wasn't home much and her mother, who seemed always home, made few appearances when we were there, so we could usually break the rules with impunity. Still, we rarely did because if we got a little out-of-hand Linda would say in a calm, steady tone that carried no anger or threat, "Please don't, you guys," occasionally adding, "If you break something, my dad'll kill me." She was far too kind, too good for me to wish any kind of misfortune on, killing or otherwise, so I was always the first to obey, but the others would soon follow suit.

Once, when we were ten and she was fourteen, we'd been rough-housing in the playroom, and they were a little slower to settle than usual after she asked us to stop. I studied her face as she watched them.

99

Terry Dalrymple

Back then, I couldn't have explained what I saw, but I felt it, felt it in the look of her silky auburn hair and her tanned face, the skin flawless and smooth as polished glass, but softer, much softer than glass, a softness in the gentle curves of her forehead, her nose, her full lips, her jaw line, her neck. I think what I felt was perfection. But her green eyes reflected something else I felt without really understanding, some deep sadness inside her.

"Come on guys," I said to my buddies as sternly as I could. "Cut it out."

She had blossomed physically that year and by summer had developed what I perceived as the body of a model, beautiful and perfect in every way. She could have passed for twenty-one, I thought, and looking back now I suspect she might have done so on occasion. But before she "turned wild," as people used to say about her, she spent most of that summer lolling around the pool. So did Stanley and I and a couple other friends. We didn't generally think much about girls back then, but I thought a lot about Linda. I would sometimes daydream about being eighteen when she would be twenty-two and when our age difference wouldn't seem so significant. I would date her then, I thought. I didn't really know what people did when they dated. I just knew I would date her if I could.

One day about mid-summer, Linda was sunbathing while we played our version of water polo. At some point, we disagreed about the score. Soon we were name-calling, then tempers flared and hands clenched and poised for an all-out fist fight. But before punches were thrown, Linda slipped into the pool, glided over to us, and laid gentle hands on the shoulders closest to her—mine and Stanley's. "Don't," she said, far more a plea than a command. "There's enough meanness in the world without you adding to it." We eased our fists down and nodded. Even after she slipped out of the pool and settled back into her lounge chair, I felt the warmth of her palm against my shoulder and wished she would have kept her hand there forever.

That incident must have nestled itself deep in my memory because it came back to me many years later, came back very suddenly and very vividly, and I wondered how such a beautiful, kind, gentle, upper-middle-class fourteen-year-old girl could have already known the extent

100

of meanness in the world. Did she hear it in a movie? Did she intuit it? Or did her father, perhaps, teach it by example? Who knows?

However she knew it, I'd guess it's a major reason she "turned wild."

And wild she did turn. Her antics became legendary. In October, after that summer we spent at her pool, she was busted for drinking under the stands at a football game, and a few months later her dad walked in on her screwing a senior in the game room, a bottle of Southern Comfort clutched in her hand during the act. At sixteen, she moved into a little country shack with a guy who had graduated two years earlier and made his living selling dope. Before her parents tracked her down, she and the guy both landed in jail. He served a little time, but as a minor she was released to the custody of her parents. She supposedly told the judge that she'd rather go to jail, but he sent her home just the same.

A few days later, Stanley called to tell me that her dad had bought a pool table, that it was off-limits to kids, but that he was out of town and she had called to say we could come play if wanted. We wanted, and I agreed to meet him there. I arrived before him, and as I approached the game room I spotted Linda out by the pool. The day was cool, and she sat lotus-style in jeans and a beige sweater, staring into the water. When I walked over and sat next to her, she glanced at me and smiled, but in her eyes I saw that same mysterious sadness I had seen two years before. She gazed back into the water. There was something I wanted to say, something I felt but had no words for. So I just sat quietly with her.

After a time, she reached across and folded her hand over mine. "Sweet Tony," she said. I blushed and we were silent again. Her perfume or skin lotion or maybe shampoo smelled of vanilla and coconut. Sitting next to her felt good.

Finally, I said, "You know what? You could be a movie star." She smiled but said nothing. "Really," I said, then after a pause, "Or a model. Or anything. You know?"

"Sweet Tony," she repeated. I felt a lump in my throat.

When Stanley arrived, I apologized, said I didn't feel like playing pool after all. I shoved my hands into my pockets and headed home.

The day Linda turned seventeen, she totaled the family car doing eighty on a residential street with a turn she couldn't quite make. She took out some poor family's living room wall and was, the police report said, so completely under the influence of drugs and alcohol as to think she had just been in a plane crash and to insist that the pilot's license be revoked. Her license, instead, was revoked, but the following summer she stole her parents' brand new Ford Crown Victoria, drove to San Antonio, sold the car to a chop-shop for twelve hundred dollars, and hitch-hiked to Santa Fe, where she was tracked down and hauled back home.

Once, at the movie theater, I bumped into her when I went for popcorn. She seemed no different to me than she ever had. I still wanted to be older, still wanted to date her. There at the concession stand, I literally bumped into her elbow, and when she turned and recognized me, she flashed a smile more beautiful and certainly more sincere than any movie star I'd ever seen.

"Hey, sweet Tony," she said and reached for my shoulders. I could smell the alcohol on her breath. "How's my favorite guy?" Braless in a vee-neck tank top, she buried my face in her cleavage when she pulled me against her in a bear hug. Then all I could feel was those soft, supple breasts against my cheek, and all I could smell was vanilla and coconut and comfort and paradise. Perfection.

Somehow, she managed to finish high school. But the day after she graduated, she ran off to Austin, where, depending on whose rumor you chose, she helped farm marijuana in a commune somewhere off Bee Cave Road, danced at a strip club on 6th Street, lived in a VW bus with a band member from the 13th Floor Elevators, starred in low-budget porn films, waitressed in a coffeehouse on 6th Street where she also read protest poetry on open-mic nights, or fucked some politician in exchange for a penthouse apartment and all the drugs she pleased. I preferred to think she modeled clothing and make-up for major companies or attended UT or volunteered for the March of Dimes. Who knows?

In any case, she stayed in Austin for a little over a year, stayed until July 19, 1969, when she returned like a phantom, showed Stanley her tits, and then disappeared forever so far as any of us knew.

Stanley was fourteen, almost fifteen, at the time. Linda's parents had given up on her, and that summer they took a long vacation to Hawaii. They hired Stanley to tend to the yard and plants while they were away. That afternoon, he stepped into their house and found Linda in the living room wearing only panties and caressing her own breasts as she danced to the psychedelic sounds of Jimi Hendrix. Stoned silly on what we later guessed must have been LSD, she giggled and said to Stanley, "Look, aren't they groovy? C'm'ere, little man. C'm'ere an' touch 'em." She grabbed him by the wrists and pressed his palms against the sweat-beaded swell of her tits. "Aren't they groovy?" He allowed as how they were, indeed, groovy, but he was so terrified by her drug-crazed behavior that he fled the house as soon as she released his wrists.

He never told his parents or hers, and she left behind only a brief note to her parents: "Rock is life. I'm hitching to Woodstock. Thanks for nothing. Peace."

In September she sent two postcards, both postmarked in Big Sur, California. The first came addressed to "My Little Minky." Most everyone called him Stanley or Mincus or sometimes Mink. Linda had been the only one ever to call him My Little Minky. He had grabbed the mail on his way in from school, a habitual act that served him well that day because he wouldn't have wanted to explain the card to his parents. I never saw it, but he told me it said, "Sorry about the boob thing. Don't be scared or scarred. I'm okay and you're okayer. Peace, Stardust." He burned the card so his parents wouldn't see it, but he did tell them that he'd gotten it and that Linda was okay and had apparently changed her name to Stardust.

Two days later, mine arrived. My dad had dropped the mail on the counter without even looking at it. My mother found it later and brought it to me in my room. Linda had obviously hand made it out of thin white cardboard. On one side she had drawn a dizzying psychedelic design with a peace sign in the middle. She addressed it to "My Sweet Tony." "I am stardust," she wrote. "You are golden. Don't ever change. Love, Stardust."

"Who is Stardust?" my mother asked, "and why does she call you my sweet Tony?"

"It's Linda," I said. "Linda Starkey. I don't know, it's just something she used to call me."

Either that answer served well enough or my mother didn't want to pry. In any case, all she said was, "That poor girl." Her voice sounded like she meant it. "She's just so wild."

I shrugged. "I guess."

My mother seemed lost in sympathy. "So pretty," she said, "with so much opportunity, so much potential, but she threw it all away."

"Maybe," I said. "But who knows?"

Nobody ever heard from Linda again, not, that is, until she wrote me thirty-three years later. She had tracked me down via the internet, I assumed, gotten my address off the university's web site. The card came there, to my department. It was postmarked in Taos, and the message was telegraphic: "My Sweet Tony, Hill Country Folk Festival. Any chance? Little Minky, too. Peace, Stardust."

I immediately called Stanley at his office in Dallas, read him the card. He was speechless.

"The festival," I said, "that starts next week, doesn't it?"

"Yeah, I think so."

"Okay, we've got to move fast."

His voice turned hesitant. "Listen, Tony, I don't know. Work's killing me, and Deanne and I just started a major renovation on the house."

I was flabbergasted. "Mincus, we've got to go. *We've got to go.*"

"I don't know. It's been a long time, you know? I wouldn't even know what to say."

"Well shit, Mincus, say hello. That's always a good place to start."

"Yeah, but listen, you know, Linda—"

"Stardust," I interrupted without even meaning to.

"Yeah, okay, Stardust. She's not exactly a bright spot in the family history, you know? She was wild. She was crazy."

"You're crazy," I said. "She loved you, man."

"I guess."

"Damn right. We're going."

He said he'd be there.

Bailey, my wife and the mother of my three beautiful children, made no protest, perhaps because I didn't mention Stardust, simply said that Mincus and I wanted to catch up, listen to some music, have a few beers. I eased the guilt of my omission by telling myself it was just curiosity. Where had she gone? What had she done? Who had she become? But in truth, I pictured Stardust as she had been years ago, smelled vanilla and coconut and comfort, and daydreamed about having gone wherever she had gone, having done whatever she had done, having become whatever she had needed to erase that sadness from her eyes.

I arrived at the hotel late Friday afternoon. I'd had no word from Stanley, and he was nowhere to be found. I grabbed a bite and then drove out to the festival, where the mass of people disheartened me. Soon the evening would darken and I'd never find Stardust in this veritable ocean of humanity. I wandered for half an hour or so, passed the arts and crafts stalls and food booths, scanned the concert crowd from behind the rows of benches on which they sat, barely listened to a group that sang Bob Dylan covers badly and their own songs even worse. Near a booth selling turquoise jewelry, a guy stopped me to ask for a light. He was an old hippie, one of those who looked like he'd never gotten the word that the sixties ended, that love was no longer free, and that "better living through chemistry" now meant a solid dose of Lipitor every day. I apologized for being lighterless, said I'd quit smoking three years before, then asked if by any chance he knew someone named Stardust. He clenched his cigarette between his teeth and stared up into the night sky as if trying to find his memory there. "I think so," he finally said. "Once, a long time ago, some-where out in Idaho or Oregon or maybe Washington." He squinted at the stars. "No, wait, I think it was Ontario." He looked back at me and took a deep drag off the still unlit cigarette. He blew the imaginary smoke into the night, then said, "Shit, man, maybe it was nowhere. Who knows?"

I thanked him for trying and took my leave. My chances of finding Stardust, I decided, would be better in the daylight, maybe mid-afternoon the next day when fewer people were around. I pondered grabbing a beer before leaving, and the few seconds I took to decide against it changed my search tactics entirely.

As I stood looking over at the beer and wine concession booth, two college-age girls passed between the booth and me. The brunette, wearing very short cut-off jeans and a bikini top dazzlingly white against her deeply tanned skin complained, "He promised. Last night he swore he'd leave a note on the message board."

"Tina," her companion said, clearly disgusted. She wore more modest shorts and a tie-dyed tee-shirt with the festival logo and name directly over her ample breasts. "Last night he just wanted to get laid. He'd have promised anything."

I wondered whether he'd been successful. I wondered if I was there for the same reason, but, not wanting to linger over that possibility, I shook the thought off. And then I wondered why I hadn't thought to look for a message board. I found it a bout fifty feet inside the entrance, where the path forked, one leg toward concessions, where I had just been, the other toward the rows of wooden benches that served as concert seating. I had passed it twice already in my wanderings.

A woman stepped up beside me and squinted at the board. Her exact age was hard to determine. Her leathery, wrinkled face could have been the face of a hard-living forty-something or a well worn fifty-something, or a fairly normal, sun-loving sixty-something. Her hair was silver gray and wispy. She wore a soiled looking granny skirt with an equally soiled white sleeveless cotton blouse that did little to disguise her braless breasts, which sagged almost onto her significantly protruding belly. She lifted a hand to brush a stray gray hair or two out of her eyes. The move revealed not only that she did not shave her armpits but that she had braided the lengthy growths in each. Apparently not finding what she looked for, she mumbled to herself and shuffled out of sight.

Until that moment, I had pictured Stardust exactly as she'd been thirty-three years before—the silky auburn hair, the beautiful face with the soft curves, the gentle green eyes filled with all that sadness. But at that moment, I realized she would be fifty-two, perhaps gray haired like this woman, her softness diminished by the wrinkles of time and sun and, perhaps, drug addiction. Who knows? I thought.

Among all the scrawled messages there, Stardust's almost immediately caught my eye when I turned my attention to the board. She had placed it smack dab in the middle of the board, a post card with a hand-drawn peace sign. In the left wedge of pie created by the design, she had written, "My Sweet Tony & (I hope) My Little Minky." The right hand wedge said, "Fri. nite picnic table by veg. tacos then front row." The bottom wedge said, "Sat. 2-4ish same table." Having run out of wedges, she had printed the final message underneath the peace sign: "Sat. nite not sure."

I scanned the row of concession stands from where I stood. Some had no signs, but one about halfway up the row had a sign painted pale green. My distance and the graying twilight made reading the lettering impossible. Still, I thought pale green a good bet for a vegetarian taco stand—if veg, indeed, meant vegetarian. I trotted up the path, then stopped short when I spotted a picnic table maybe thirty feet across from the green-lit booth. My heart pounded. The table sat underneath a huge oak, which dimmed the little remaining light even more. Two figures sat on the far side, their backs to the table top as they looked, I assumed, toward the distant stage. I approached from behind. The sound of my shoes on gravel must have caught the man's attention. He turned, saw me standing there, nudged her shoulder with his elbow, and nodded back toward me. She turned and squinted in the dimness. Then she squealed.

"Tony!" she yelled. "Sweet Tony! My sweet, sweet Tony!" Before she finished saying it, she had risen, swung herself across the table, and flung her arms around my neck. I felt paralyzed. I felt numb. And I was struck totally and completely dumb. At that moment I don't believe I could see or smell anything, and I could feel only her arms squeezing my neck and hear only her voice saying my name, the voice a bit deeper, perhaps, but still that same voice from my past, Stardusts's lovely voice. She released me. "God," she said, "it's so good to see you."

"Yeah," I managed, then, concentrating hard to make my brain and mouth work, "Hello."

She laughed. "Well hello."

"It's a good place to start, right?" I said.

"Yeah, Tony, it's a great place to start. Listen, say hello to Jimmy." By then the man had walked around the table and stood next to her. She laid a hand on his shoulder. "Jimmy, this is Tony, Tony Hawkins. My sweet Tony." The little light that reached his face revealed that it was deeply tanned and sun-wrinkled. His hair looked dark and appeared to be pulled back into a ponytail. He had no paunch, none of the softness that typically overtakes us at a certain age. He was slender and taut, wiry maybe. "Tony, this is Jimmy Lark." We shook hands and the strength of his grip made me wince.

He grinned broadly. "Damn good to meet you, Tony."

"Yeah," I said, relieved when he released the grip. "You too."

"Listen," he said, "it's hot as hell. You want a drink?"

"Sure. A beer would be great." He nodded and headed off to get it. When he moved from in front of me, I noticed two water bottles standing in sweat rings on the table. Stardust traced my line of sight.

"Clean and sober," she said. "Twenty-seven years."

"You know what, Jimmy," I called after him. He turned to look back. "Just a water would be good." He gave me the thumbs up and went on.

Stardust slapped my shoulder. "Tony, you can have a beer."

"Water's good," I said. "Water's great."

"Always Sweet Tony." She smiled, then suddenly stepped up and threw her arms around me again. That time, I hugged back. We squeezed hard, and I pushed my nose and mouth into her hair. I smelled vanilla and coconut, though later guessed that was memory at work. She stepped back. "You look great, Tony."

"You too. Mind if I stare?"

"Stare all you want. I can't get enough of you into my eyes, either."

We concentrated on each other's faces, I careful not to start with her eyes. I had to look, had to know, but wasn't ready for disappointment if I found that same sadness lingering there. So I started with her hair, still shoulder length and for the most part still auburn, just streaked with gray here and there. Her face had retained the same softness I remembered in the gentle curves of her forehead, her nose, her full lips, her jaw line, her neck. Her tan complexion was lovely, though not quite as smooth and flawless as it had once been. Little wrinkle rays of crows' feet branched from the corners of her eyes and parentheses enclosed her mouth, all of them what my mother used to call laugh lines when she developed them. That thought inspired me to go to the eyes. They shone back at me with excitement, with love, with happiness, with peacefulness, with perfection.

She eased into me for a more gentle hug than before and said softly, "Really, you look fantastic, Tony."

"You, too," I said.

"Did you see enough?" she asked.

"Never, but it'll do for now."

Jimmy arrived with my bottle of water. I thanked him but avoided eye contact, embarrassed that he caught us hugging so tenderly. I took a swig. Stardust, apparently not at all embarrassed, slipped her arm around Jimmy's waist in the same gentle way she had just hugged me. "This guy," she said, "is the one who got me straight."

Jimmy grinned, then shrugged. "You're a smart girl. You'd have done it on your own sooner or later."

"Maybe. Who knows? Anyway, you got me there sooner." She stretched to kiss his temple.

I felt a twinge of jealousy that this man, this stranger to me, had been exactly what I always thought I wanted to be for her. But stronger was the feeling of relief that she had found whatever it was she needed.

"That's great, Stardust" I said. "I'm really glad you got there."

She and Jimmy looked at each other and broke into full-fledged laughter. "I'm sorry," she said. "It just sounds funny, you calling me Stardust."

"Why's it funny?"

"It's what we named our company, but it hasn't been my name since I quit smoking dope and dropping acid."

I'm not sure if felt disappointed or just confused. "But your post card, and the note on the message board. . . ."

"Yeah," she said. "See, I don't use my maiden name ever. Never, not for any reason. And I figured you could have known twenty Lindas in the past thirty-three years. And the last name, Lark, wouldn't mean anything to you. But I figured odds were good you'd never known another Stardust."

"Never," I smiled. "Never have, never will."

"Come on, let's sit. Tell us about your life."

We sat at the picnic table, the two of them on one side, I on the other. My conversation was awkward at first, unsure as I was about how Jimmy would view this reunion. But he was friendly and seemed genuinely happy to meet me, genuinely glad I had come to see Linda. I loosened quickly, and we talked comfortably for half an hour. Linda said she wanted to meet Bailey and all my kids. They had no children. They had met twenty-eight years before, and he was the one who helped her get straight. They married a couple years later, and for twenty years they had owned a business in Taos called Stardust Gardens which, as she described it laughingly, was a hippie-ish/new age-ish/xeriscape-ish gift shop/green-house/landscape business. Apparently, they had been successful with it.

Jimmy, it turned out, also had a little acoustic band, a trio simply called Lark, and they were playing at the festival that night. He excused himself to meet his band mates backstage.

Linda took my hand and led me down some stone steps to the other pathway. We walked to a front-row bench where she had draped a blanket to save spots for us. She covered room enough for three. She sat close up against me and folded the blanket onto the third space on her other side.

"Jimmy's a nice guy," I said.

She smiled. "Yeah, he's a really good man." She looked in the direction he had gone, almost as if she could still see him there. "And so are you." She turned, smiled, looked hard into my eyes. "You know," she said, "I almost came back to find you once."

I laid my hand on her shoulder. "I wish you had."

"It was four, maybe five years after I left home. It was before I met Jimmy." Her vague smile fell slowly into a vague frown. "That was a bad time, a really bad time. And this one afternoon I sat by a river—the Green River up in Utah—and watched the water rolling by and thought about jumping in, rolling with it, never coming out."

"That *was* a bad time," I said. "But I don't think it was the first time."

"No. In fact as I sat there, I remembered a time when I sat by my swimming pool with about the same thoughts in my head. And then you came along and sat next to me. Do you remember?"

"Better than you might imagine."

She finally turned to look at me, the vague smile returning. "That day by the Green River, I wanted to find you. I wanted you to sit by me again."

"I would have."

"Of course you would have, sweet Tony. And I guess in my mind you did." She patted my leg, but then pulled herself abruptly erect, as if pulling herself up out of that memory. "Hey," she said, "do you think he'll come?" She gestured to the blanket-covered space beside her. "Do you think Minky will make it?"

A little slower to pull myself back from that day by the swimming pool, I must have seemed unsure because she followed with, "He won't, will he? He won't come."

I had gained the present by then and said, "Of course he will. Of course he'll come."

"I don't know," she said. She looked up the hill where a few booths were still open, their dim lights soft and seemingly as tentative as she sounded. "My family—everyone, really—from back then, they're not . . ." Her hands lay folded in her lap. She looked down at them, her lips pressed tightly together as she tried to find the right words. "They don't. . ."

"Linda," I said, "you are stardust. You are golden. He loves you. He'll be here."

"Maybe," she said. "Who knows?" Then smiled again. "Anyway, you're here."

"I couldn't not be."

"Sweet Tony. Always and forever sweet Tony."

"Maybe not always. You've missed a few years."

"You have an old soul and a tender heart. You were always sweet Tony back then, and you're the same sweet Tony right now. I know it."

"If I was, and if I am, you get some credit." I studied her profile. "You know," I said, "I'm the better for having known you."

She looked at me and smiled. "Always sweet Tony." She paused, then cocked her head and said, "Tony, do you want to make love?"

It wasn't coquettish. It wasn't flirtatious. It wasn't a come-on or an invitation. It was a direct, sincere question, pure and simple. And its tone kept it from surprising or embarrassing me. It was, in fact, a good question, a reasonable question, an important question. I looked at the still-soft curves of her face, remembered the first time I had noticed them. I looked at the swell of her breasts beneath her blouse, remembered the time she had bear-hugged my face into her cleavage, remembered the way those soft breasts had felt against my chest when she hugged me earlier. I remembered how I used to daydream about her, even long after she disappeared. But what struck most emphatically was a memory I had never before recognized. In all those years, none of those daydreams ever included sex. In every one, no matter where we were or what we were doing, we were simply together and the sadness was gone from her eyes.

Then, there at the festival, I looked directly into her eyes and said, "I guess not."

She smiled and patted my shoulder. "Good," she said. "Neither do I." We both laughed. She leaned in and kissed my cheek, her lips warm and soft and gentle against my skin.

111

Something clattered on the stage and we turned our attention that way. Lost in conversation with her, I had been oblivious to the last few songs of the previous band and to the fact that they had vacated the stage and Jimmy's band was almost finished setting up. We watched their final preparations. Then Linda slipped her hand into mine and we sat quietly listening to the music. And sitting next to her felt good.

III. Therapy

Therapy

Plenty of you out there know what it's like to be abandoned by a spouse. You get depressed, maybe you drink, maybe you obsess about the best ways to kill yourself. You let yourself go. You feel like hell and you look like hell. Eventually, if you're lucky, you pull yourself out of it, or someone pulls you out. You clean up, you lose weight, you put yourself out there again and hope against hope that all that effort pays off.

That's my story, a fairly common one, so common , perhaps, that it's not worth the telling. But maybe—and I can't be sure about this, but just maybe—the Lynn part of my story is unique. So here it is.

I was a firm believer in the miracle of romance and love and devotion until the day I startled my wife, Sharon, and myself by arriving home and finding her curled up with a man ten years her junior on the king-sized bed I had not finished paying for. After her initial gasp, she stood up calm, composed, naked, kissed me gently on the cheek, and said good-bye. Within six months she had legal custody of our two children and moved three hundred miles away with that young stud.

I succumbed to depression, then alcohol, then the obsession with the best ways to kill myself. By the time the company psychiatrist cleared the haze, I had lost much of my colleagues' respect, most of my friends' sympathy, and all of my faith in what I had once perceived as the miracle of romance and love and devotion.

But even in a world devoid of romance and love and devotion—perhaps especially in such a world—sexual urges prevail. Once I cleaned up, prevail they did. But after nearly seventeen years of marriage and slightly before turning forty-five, finding someone with whom to satisfy those urges proved problematic. Available younger women I knew wanted romance; available older women, mostly divorcees, wanted, love and devotion. I could offer none of those. But I still needed sex. And then I saw the writing on the wall.

On a Friday evening after work, I stopped at one of the finer restaurants in town. I had worked late to finish up a rather large project, felt quite satisfied with it, and so rewarded myself with a fat, juicy filet mignon, medium rare. It was there, in the second stall of the men's restroom, that I saw the writing on the wall.

FOR A MIRACULOUS TIME, CALL LYNN: 923-1447. So said the writing on the wall.

I had never believed much in such messages, written, I guessed, as some kind of practical joke or maybe as some kind of revenge by jilted lovers. But this one seemed different: the classiness of the place where I read it, the artistry of the hand that wrote it, the poetic nature of its content—nothing as unimaginative as "For a good time, call Lynn" or as base as "Lynn gives good head." No, instead it said, FOR A MIRACULOUS TIME, CALL LYNN.

Most likely my desperation did the reasoning, but by the time I reached home I had convinced myself that the message was legitimate, and, God knows, I needed a miraculous time.

I stared at the phone for a good five minutes. I mean, seriously, what do you say to a woman whose number you found on a bathroom wall? Nothing came to me. Still, I finally wiped my sweaty palms on my pants, took a deep breath, and dialed.

"Lynn speaking." A soft, smooth, satiny voice. "Well?" She waited for an answer, but I could think of none. "How can I help you?"

I wiped my free palm on my shirt front, switched the receiver to the dry palm, wiped the other. "Okay," I said. "Do you . . . Could we . . . I wondered if . . . ." My head was empty or else so full that I could make no sense of what was there.

"What is it? What do you wonder?"

In one long sentence without pauses, I told her my name and my age and my job and my hobbies (which I invented on the spot) and few of my likes and dislikes, and I told her I had heard nice things about her. My breath exhausted, I gasped for more and added, "And I was just wondering if we could meet sometime."

"Yes," she said. "I'd like to meet you."

"You would?"

"Absolutely."

If she was going to be that easy, I figured I'd push my luck. "Tonight?"

"Yes, I'm free tonight."

I fumbled for a pencil, scrawled the address she gave, forgot to say good-bye.

When she opened the door, I literally gasped. Lynn was utterly stunning. You'll think I'm making this up, I know, or maybe that I'm plagiarizing some formulaic romance novel, but I swear it's true. At least ten years younger than I, she wore a white satin blouse with no bra and dark blue designer jeans so tight she might have painted them on. Her freshly washed sandy-blonde hair spilled over her shoulders and outlined a fashion-model face. She had large, almond-shaped eyes, blue-gray, canopied by long lashes, her eyelids tinted with a whisper of pale pink make-up. Pale pink lip gloss highlighted her full lips, which curved smoothly into a bright smile.

"Welcome," she said, and her tone said she meant it. I shoved a bouquet of multi-colored carnations toward her.

She guided me into her living room and offered me a seat on her white velour couch. She arranged the carnations between two scented candles on the coffee table before us. Her breasts swayed sensually beneath the white satin blouse. She poured two goblets of White Zinfandel. When she set the carafe down, its remaining contents lapped at its sides and reflected the glow of candlelight. She sat close to me on the couch, her long slender arm laid along the backrest, not quite touching me. We each sipped the wine.

"So," she said, "tell me about yourself."

My lips twitched nervously when I smiled back at her. I shrugged. "Not much to tell."

She laid her long smooth fingers against the back of my neck. "What about your ex-wife?" She said it gently, soothingly. I shrugged. She massaged my neck and smiled. "It's okay. Talk to me. It's good therapy."

I talked. I told her everything. She listened quietly, sympathetically, stroked my neck with her long pink fingernails, poured more wine. Once started, I couldn't stop. I told her things even my psychiatrist hadn't heard, and with every word spoken I felt lighter, giddier, happier than I'd been since catching Sharon *in flagrante,* maybe even since well before that time. When I finished, she kissed my forehead, took my hand, and led me into her bedroom.

Kneeling by the bed while I sat on its edge, she removed my shoes. Like the living room, her bedroom glowed from the light of scented candles. The bare walls, painted high-gloss pale pink, appeared to pulsate gently in the flickering light. She massaged my feet.

On a night stand next to us, her sleek push-button phone jerked me out of my reverie. She smiled up at me, still massaging, and left the phone to her answering machine, the volume of which was turned all the way down.

Lynn removed her own shoes, stretched out fully clothed on the white satin sheets, pressed my head against those wonderfully supple breasts, and massaged my scalp with those magic fingers.

The muscles in my head and face collapsed from the massage.

"I'm glad you found me," she said.

We did not make love. We simply lay together all night on her satin sheets, the satin bedspread folded neatly at the foot of the bed. We talked quietly, touched lightly, laughed often. I didn't miss the sex. She provided enough—more than enough—incredible sensations with her fingernails against my scalp, her breasts against my ear, her breath against my cheek, her sweet smell everywhere.

I left her apartment just at sunrise. As I replayed the night in my mind, I watched the bright orange arch of the sun ease slowly above the horizon.

I know this doesn't sound credible, but, again, I swear it's true. And I know I sound unbelievably naive, which perhaps I was. I never questioned why she so unhesitatingly accepted my invitation to meet, and I never questioned why a woman of her age and beauty would treat a man like me so romantically, so tenderly, even before she really knew him. What can I say? I was smitten. If those questions had crossed my mind, I would have dismissed them immediately. Why had she treated me the way she had? Well, why not?

I slept a little when I got home from our night together, and spent most of the afternoon propped up in bed, replaying our evening again and again in my head. About five, I called her. Her answering machine picked up. I told her she was miraculous. I said I wanted to see her again. I said please, please, please call me back. She did not call back that night, and about ten I tried again but left no message. After a sleepless night, I called once more. Again I got her answering machine. "Please," I said.

Late that afternoon, she called. "How do you feel?" she asked.

"Top of the world."

"Good."

"When can I see you again?"

Several beats passed before she answered. "Listen, why don't you call someone. Someone you know. A woman."

I felt as if I'd just been slugged in the gut. "What?"

"A woman," she said. "Someone you know."

"I know you, Lynn."

"The thing is," she said, "I'll be unavailable for awhile."

"Unavailable?"

"Yes. Out-of-pocket."

"Out-of-pocket?"

"Please," she said. "Call someone."

Sure that she was about to hang up, I blurted, "I'm coming over. I'll be there in an hour." I hung up before she could.

I plopped into a chair, shoved my face into my palms. I'll be unavailable, she had said. Out-of-pocket. Call someone, she had said. Someone you know. A woman. Names and images of women flitted involuntarily through my mind. The younger ones looking for romance, the older ones looking for love and devotion. My evening with Lynn had left me feeling that I might again be capable of believing in such things. But I wanted them with her. And who would have me anyway? I had alienated so many colleagues and friends and acquaintances. Who was left?

Well, there was Marsha, a divorced office-mate. She was plain but shapely enough, and she had been kind throughout my depressed, drunken, suicidal days. She had offered an encouraging word here and a pat on the back there, and she always smiled when we greeted each other. And there was Leslie, a friend of my ex-wife's before our break-up. A little younger than I, about Lynn's age, she had divorced two years before we did, and we had more-or-less lost touch with her. She was pretty enough but flat-chested and a little on the skinny side. She had called me, I began to remember, several times after my divorce. She had asked how I was, and I had lied and said I was fine. She had reminded me that she'd been through divorce, too. She had said if I needed to talk about it she would listen. I had thanked her but said no, I didn't need to talk. And there was that waitress at the restaurant where I found Lynn's number. She was, I judged, about Leslie's age but with a much fuller build and a lovely, sincere smile. We had chatted in spurts as she took my order, served me, and checked on me a couple of times. She had been pleasant, easy to chat with in those few moments, and seemed genuinely interested in what I said. I couldn't remember if she wore a wedding ring.

Perhaps there were others, but I shook off the distraction and changed clothes hurriedly.

I arrived at Lynn's door forty-five minutes after calling her. She didn't answer my knock. I tried the knob. It was unlocked. After a brief search, I found her in the bedroom. She wore what appeared to be a man's light blue, button-up cotton shirt without, of course, a bra. She lay crossways on her bed, the sole of her left foot flat against the satin sheets, the knee up. Her right leg crossed over the left, its foot dangling, only the toes touching the bed. The tail of her blouse fell open below the last button and revealed white panties. She propped her head on a pillow, across which her hair washed carelessly. She held her sleek telephone receiver to her right ear. When I entered she jerked the receiver from her ear and cupped it against her chest, tightening her shirt against her otherwise bare breasts. "You're early," she said. I didn't speak, couldn't speak. Without hesitation, she added, "But you're welcome." She patted the bed, an invitation to lie beside her, and lifted the receiver back to her ear. I longed to comply, to lie beside her, my head burrowed where the receiver had been, my scalp tingling as her pink fingernails smoothed my hair. I longed for a slow-motion replay of the night we spent together. But I simply stood looking down at her.

"Yes," she said into the receiver, "I'd like to meet you. Can I call you back?" She waited for an answer, then said, "Yes, I promise." She set the receiver in its cradle and looked up at me. "I guess you know."

I shrugged. "Not really."

"Do you want to?"

"Not really."

She rose from the bed, held out her arms. I stepped into her and we hugged tightly. She kissed my cheek and began to pull back, but I pulled her close again, pressed my lips against hers, and kissed her deeply. She didn't resist.

"I love you," I said when I released her.

She placed her palm against my cheek and smiled. "And I you."

"Somehow," I said, "I believe you."

"People shouldn't be lonely," she said. "They shouldn't hurt."

I scanned her beautiful face, her breasts outline by the blue cotton shirt, her smooth, long legs. "But why you?"

"Why not?" she said. "Because I can," she said.

I nodded. "So—" I hesitated, studied her face. "—how much?"

She hissed at me, scowled. "I don't charge."

"Well, then why?"

She shrugged. "Call it an avocation. A hobby, maybe. It's therapy."

I took one last, long look at all of her loveliness, then turned, walked out of the bedroom and toward the front door. She followed. When I neared the door, she called my name. I paused, turned.

"If you ever need to," she said, "you can call me."

I nodded and turned back toward the door, but when I reached it, I turned again. " I hope I never need to."

She smiled and blew me a kiss. "Me, too," she said.

I blew a kiss back and left her house.

Snow Angel

A sound like the brushing of soft wings against the window roused Aaron Gardner from the haze of half-sleep. He arose gently so as not to waken his wife, Darla, from her untroubled sleep. He stepped carefully through the darkness toward the window, shivering more from fear than from the cold. At the window, he paused, breathed deeply, then parted the curtains slightly with his palms. His rigid muscles relaxed as he squinted out into his brightly moonlit yard and saw nothing. No snow. No angel. Only the winter-browned grass and a few of Kevin and Michelle's toys scattered carelessly about. Only things that belonged there. Only things that fit.

Snow did not fit. Not in Brownsville, Texas, where the largest recorded snowfall was what meteorologists called "a trace." Angels did not fit. Not anywhere. Nor did the risen dead nor the love of another woman, a woman not his wife.

Aaron leaned his forehead against the cold glass. He forced a chuckle. He thought he might cry. Or vomit. He wanted a drink.

* * *

The night before had been wet and cold and black, the moon smothered by thick, dark clouds. At midnight or past, he had not wanted to stop. But the woman looked miserable, huddled in a thin sweater, leaning against her Toyota, its hood open. He pulled up beside her, leaned across to inch open the passenger side window.

"Can I help?"

"Please," she said and reached for the door handle. Trying the locked door, she leaned down to peer in the window. "May I?" He hesitated, distracted by the jolt he felt. Something in her voice. Something almost but not quite familiar. A jolt inside him somewhere, a place he could not locate, a place he did not recognize. "Please?" she said.

He flipped the lock up and she jerked open the door and tumbled in. "God," she said, slamming the door and then shuddering as she settled into the seat hugging herself for warmth. "It's freezing. I'm freezing." Her teeth literally chattered. He had never heard teeth literally chatter.

"I have another coat," he said. He turned on the dome light, reached into the back seat for the coat. He shuddered when he first touched it, almost did not pick it up. But, hearing her teeth chatter, he gritted his own, grabbed the coat, and hurriedly shoved it into her lap.

"You're a dream," she said, and he thought it might be true. Wished it were true. Wished the whole day had been a dream. Lorenzo Cantu's prediction of snow. Old Mrs. Delecroe's reported angel-sighting. The coat of a dead friend whose mother insisted he would return. None of it belonged. None of it fit.

And now, this woman. The jolt. A jolt that recurred when he looked at her in the dim glow of the dome light. Her dark, wet hair, clinging limply to her cheeks and neck. Her pale, smooth face, its features thin, delicate. The smile into which she tried to force her blue, trembling lips. The crescent of white shoulder where her damp sweater sagged.

"I'm Maggie Dillard. And you're in the road," she said. "Should you pull over?" Despite her shivering, her voice was steady, calm, warm.

"Do you know what's wrong?" He nodded toward her car.

"No idea. It stalled at fifty miles an hour three times tonight. This time it won't start. It's a mystery."

"There are no mysteries," he said more emphatically than he intended. He shrugged apologetically. "But I'm no mechanic."

"That's okay. Could you just take me into Harlingen?"

She seemed to have warmed quickly. Her teeth no longer chattered. She smiled.

"Sure." He turned off the dome light and thought he could feel the darkness move in to replace it, wrap around him, around her, sealing them inside the car, the car the only thing separating the darkness inside from the darkness outside, the only thing keeping them from floating into universal darkness, void.

I love you, he almost said. The jolt.

* * *

He returned from the window to the bed and sat cross-legged facing Darla. "I love you," he whispered. He admired the fine lines of her pale face, the fine dark hair that tumbled across her pillow, the apparent innocence of her sleep. "I love you," he said, and he wanted it to be true. Knew it was true. And knew that, loving her, he could love no one else. It did not fit. "I love you. I don't want to love anyone else. I love you." But each time he said it, Maggie Dillard's face floated before him. Floated between him and Darla. Smiled at him from within the swirl of a snow storm, angels dipping in and out of the picture on crystal-feathered wings, touching gravestones from beneath which rose bodies of the wakened dead.

* * *

It had started with the phone call two mornings before. Ace Stone, Michael Stone's father, had not even started with hello.

"Jesus, Aaron," he had said. "He jumped. He just jumped."

"Ace, what is it? What are you talking about?"

"Michael. He's dead."

"Dead?"

"Jesus! He just jumped." Ace's voice reflected utter bewilderment rather than sorrow.

"What do you mean? What happened?"

"He was patching the roof for me. Whistling. Aaron, he was whistling and singing and teasing me about being too cheap to hire a professional."

"What happened? Did he fall?"

"He jumped, goddamn it!"

"But why?"

"I don't know. Was he on drugs, Aaron? I thought you'd know. Was he crazy?"

"I don't know. No, I don't think so. He was happy. I think he was happy. Was Jenny there?"

"Jenny and the kids, too. He stood up and waved at them and Myrna and me. He was smiling. And whistling! Then he said, real calm and matter of fact, 'God, the fascination of jumping.' And he did it. He just jumped. Head first onto the patio!"

"Jesus!" Aaron heard his own voice as an echo of Mr. Stone's. The bewilderment. The death did not bewilder him. Death was a fact. It fit. It was unpleasant, but it fit. But the manner of death, there was the deformity. "He was happy. I'm sure he was happy."

"'Fascination,' he said. 'The fascination of jumping,' for Christ's sake. What is that? What does that mean?"

"I don't know." But he had heard it before, he suddenly recalled. A similar fascination. Twenty years ago in Vietnam, where they had met. Wallowing in a shallow, muddy hole, ducking bullets from unseen strangers in the dark, in the rain. *Sometimes*, Michael had said, *sometimes I want to stand up.*

You're crazy.

No. I mean, sometimes I just want to stand up. You know?

He did not know. It made no sense. It did not fit.

"There's a reason," he said, unsure, because of the silence, if Ace remained on the phone. "There has to be a reason. I only wish I knew what it was."

* * *

And he wished he knew what it was about Maggie Dillard.

"I really appreciate this," she said.

He had not been talking. The darkness, his sense of the void beyond the car, consumed his attention. That, and the sense that the two of them were sealed together both within it and against it. That, and the fear that if he spoke at all he would say, *I love you.* When she spoke, he concentrated carefully on his reply. "It's no problem, really. Harlingen is on my way."

"To?"

"Brownsville. I— we, my wife and kids and I—live in Brownsville."

"You're out late for a Brownsville family man."

"I've been to a friend's funeral in McAllen. Stayed with his family as long as I could." Not quite true. He had planned to spend the night. But Myrna Stone's talk about her son's return had finally driven him away. "And you?"

"I guess I'm out late for a Laredo single woman." She laughed, a sincere, spontaneous laugh that made him smile despite the discomfort he felt in her presence. The jolt, the feelings he so immediately had for her, were not right, did not fit. Their pleasantness, their warmth, disturbed him. "I work for a real estate chain. Got a late start for a conference in Harlingen. Then the car problems." She reached across and patted his shoulder. "Thanks for stopping," she said, squeezing the shoulder, and then, "You're a good man."

He felt the warmth of her hand even through his thick coat, a warmth that spread across his back and down his chest. The wind seemed to howl around the windows, and even the light mist seemed loud against the windshield. The center stripe blurred in the headlights. He slowed the car, glanced across at her. "Do I know you?"

She laughed again. "Sure. We just met."

"No, I mean have we met before?"

"There's an original line."

"But I'm serious."

Her voice became suddenly quieter, somber. "I wish we had," she said.

* * *

"Darla," he whispered, gently kissing her cheek. She did not stir. "Darla." He needed to tell her that he loved her, that he had always loved her, that he always would love her. He ached to tell her . . . to tell her what? That he did not believe Lorenzo Cantu's prediction of snow. That he did not—could not—believe in angels or in the risen dead. That he could never love another woman, a woman not his wife.

Darla sighed heavily and squirmed into a new position. Her breath was slow and warm. He touched her, felt the warmth of her smooth flesh. Felt the innocence of her sleep. Yearned for just such sleep himself.

* * *

He stumbled out of the house early the morning of the funeral, still baffled, confused, dazed by the news, still turning it over and over in his head to find some answer, some explanation. The unusually bitter air stung his cheeks, his eyes.

"I seen an angel," old Mrs. Delecroe hollered from next door. He heard, but did not register her voice until he glanced across at her doorstep. Dressed in a pink bathrobe and fuzzy pink slippers, she stood with her hands uplifted and gazed toward the low, gray sky.

"Mrs. Delecroe," he called, "you'll freeze to death."

She lowered her gaze toward him, and even from that distance he could see the strangeness of her eyes. Ordinarily hidden behind thick-lensed bifocals, they were now bare, and although they looked glazed from not blinking they shone with more vivacity, more youth, than he had ever seen in her.

"I seen an angel," she said and then looked back toward the sky. "White it was, with a child's pink face. And wings. Crystal wings delicate as a butterfly's."

The frozen mist on the grass crunched beneath his feet, a sound he had not heard in all his seven years in Brownsville. "Mrs. Delecroe," he said when he reached her. "Please go inside. It's too cold." He gently clutched her arm, but she seemed not to notice.

"Smiling down at me it was. Right outside my window. Just floating there, gentle as a baby."

"Come on," he said and tried to ease her toward the door. She remained firm, as if already frozen in place. "Will you go inside?"

"Lacy, crystal wings. Shining they were. Shimmering."

"Can you hear me? Please go in."

"An angel. The mystery of heaven."

"No, Mrs. Delecroe. There are no angels. There is no mystery. Maybe you saw a bird. Were you wearing your glasses?"

"It's coming back. I know it will return."

He sighed, patted her shoulder, and returned to his house to alert Darla to keep watch over the old woman.

* * *

As a child in Iowa, he had learned to make snow angels from Mrs. Pipkin, an elderly woman next door. To lie in the deep, soft snow, arms spread and moving like the gentle flapping of wings, legs moving together and apart. Then to stand up carefully so as not to mar the image. An image imprinted in the snow. A pure white image of a robed body with delicate wings. Although his mother thought Mrs. Pipkin too old for such cavorting, he and Mrs. Pipkin would play in the snow for hours, he usually tiring before she. His cheeks burning from the cold, his fingers stiff, almost unbendable, they would go into her kitchen to warm themselves with hot chocolate and popcorn. The scent of spices, fruits, and homemade bread filled the kitchen.

Anytime he felt sad or confused, he visited her there in her kitchen. There, sipping hot chocolate, crunching popcorn or cookies, drinking in the wonderful scents, feeling her warm, wrinkled hand on his head or cheek or shoulder—there, everything was right. She was his center, his balance.

* * *

Darla and their children provided his center now. His balance. He felt desperately the need for her voice, her touch. But, unwilling to disturb her further, to waken her and make her part of his craziness, he again eased out of bed. Again, he checked the window. No snow. No angel. No Michael Stone come back from the dead for his coat. He shuddered at the thought. He had left the coat with Maggie.

* * *

In a dim corner of the Holiday Inn bar in Harlingen, they drank together. She a gin and tonic, he black coffee. The bar remained quiet except for an occasional flurry of laughter from one of the two small, very drunken groups of people still there. Despite the laughter and the infrequent attention of the weary looking waitress, he felt secluded, alone with Maggie. The dim candlelight reflected in her dark, shiny eyes. Her soft voice like the soothing touch of old Mrs. Pipkin's wrinkled hand. She laughed with him about Lorenzo Cantu's prediction of snow. Touched his hand when he spoke of Michael Stone's death. Frowned philosophically when he told of Mrs. Delecroe's angel.

"Maybe she saw it," she said.

He chuckled. "In her head."

"Does that make it less real?"

"Yes." He sipped his coffee, felt its steam rise warm into his face, heard laughter, as if through a wall, from one of the drunken groups. "I don't know," he said, looking down into his cup. "I don't want to get old. To lose control like that." He suddenly felt like crying and did not know why.

"Hey," she said, and her warm, slender hand cupped his chin, tilted his head so that he looked at her. "Control isn't all it's cracked up to be."

He took her hand from his chin, held it. And he felt as if he had done so all his life. As if their hands fit perfectly together. One of the drunken groups arose noisily from their table and staggered out, leaning heavily on one another. Maggie laughed. He smiled, looked at the smooth white crescent of flesh where her sweater still drooped off her shoulder, squeezed her hand. He lay his other hand on her forearm, rubbed it gently.

"Aaron," she said softly, "are you trying to seduce me?"

He stopped rubbing. "I wish I could." The jolt. He had meant to say something else. To deny it. To make a joke of it.

"You could," she said.

He released her hand, leaned back in his chair, smiled nervously. "Control," he said. "Control."

* * *

At the funeral he had been less controlled than simply numb, unbelieving. That Michael was dead, he sadly accepted. That he had dived head first from a roof onto a concrete patio for no apparent reason, he could not understand, could not accept. He stood beside Ace at the grave site, both of them silent, staring blankly at the casket soon to be lowered into the earth, out of sight but not out of mind. Jenny and Michael's children cried quietly. Myrna wept uncontrollably.

Back at the house, she calmed, sat quietly staring with red, glazed eyes from him to Ace to Jenny and the children. He wanted to say something to make them understand. To make himself understand. Like them, he sat stiff, silent. Myrna looked old, her face drawn and pale. Old, as he remembered Mrs. Pipkin, but without the warmth, without the energy. Pitiful, as he had seen Mrs. Delecroe, but without the childish gleam of wonder in her eyes.

The furnace ran steadily, turned up high against the unusual cold outside. Too high. Stifling. Oppressive. He rubbed his sweaty palms on his pants, turned to Jenny to say something, anything to break the dreadful silence. But before he could think of what to say, Myrna spoke quietly.

"I'm worried about Michael." She looked beyond them all, toward the window. "He's a grown man, I know, but I'm worried about him. It's so cold out."

"Myrna," Ace began, but she seemed not hear and continued.

"He should be home by now. It's cold and late. Shouldn't he be home by now?"

"Myrna," and for the first time, Ace's voice cracked. "He's dead. We buried him. He's dead."

She arose and moved trance-like to the front window. She pushed the curtains back and looked out. "It's very cold. I'm worried. He'll be home soon." She allowed Ace to lead her back to her chair. "He's coming back," she said. "He'll be back soon."

Aaron shivered despite the close heat he thought might suffocate him. Snow, Lorenzo Cantu had said. An angel, Mrs. Delecroe had said. Mystery. Mystery and wonder. Michael Stone had jumped. He had simply, calmly jumped. The heat, the silence, the tension in the room pushed down on him, made breathing difficult. And he felt the several feet of earth pushing down on Michael's casket, sealing him from the world beyond, an unfamiliar world, a world that no longer existed for him. For Michael. For him. He suddenly feared the window toward which Myrna again shuffled. Feared it, and what lay beyond.

"Let's eat," Ace said.

They poked at the chicken casserole brought by a neighbor, their forks clinking dully against their plates, none of them eating more than a bite or two. They managed to talk a little. About the weather mostly.

Occasionally about Michael, but never about his death. And through it all, Myrna continually paced from the table to the front window, peered out, turned sadly to say, "No. Only a passing car."

Tense, he watched her. Wanted to stop her, to scream at her, *He's dead, gaddamn it!* And he feared her. Feared that she might turn from the window smiling, announcing Michael's return.

"Ace, I have to go." He apologized, made excuses for not staying the night as planned. The bitter wind was a relief when he opened the door, but the darkness was somehow frightening. So complete. He hesitated, then stepped out.

"Wait," Myrna called from another room. "Aaron, please wait." She ran to him, Michael's coat held in front of her like a sacrificial offering. "He might come to you. It's so cold." She handed him the coat.

"Myrna," he said, "he's not—"

"He's coming," she said. "Please."

He shuddered and took the coat.

* * *

Mrs. Pipkin had died in front of him. He had just sipped his hot chocolate, burned his tongue, smiled at the sweet taste of chocolate and melted marshmallow. Standing behind her chair, she suddenly coughed. Spit dribbled down her chin. She clutched her side, crumpled to the floor.

And then, shivering in the snow outside her door, hugging his mother's waist, he had listened to the shriek of the ambulance. Had watched the emergency medical team, their coats crisp and whiter than the snow, roll her out on the bright steel gurney, her slender body shrouded and strapped.

"She's dead," one of the men said.

Even then, even at ten years old, he understood death. It was sad. It was hard and cold. And it was final. Still, it could be explained. It was right. It fit.

Two weeks later, she returned.

He watched from his upstairs window as his father, who had volunteered to pick her up at the hospital, pushed her wheelchair up the walk, now clear of snow. Watched as his father unlocked her door, as she stood up and walked, with great difficulty, inside.

He had refused to visit her in the hospital. She was dead. He had watched her die. He refused to visit her at home. And when she hobbled to his house occasionally, he hid behind the locked door of his bedroom, pressing the heels of his hands against his ears to blot out the muffled conversation below.

* * *

At the door to her motel room, Maggie Dillard stood tiptoe and kissed his cheek. "Maybe you're right," she said. "Maybe we have met before."

"I'd remember you."

"Anyway, I wish we had." Still on tiptoe. Her cheek brushing his. Her breath warm. Her lips moving slowly toward his.

He could have hugged her. Wanted to. Could have kissed her forever there in the hall, forgetting that anyone or anything else existed. Wanted to forget.

He stepped back, extended his hand. "Thank you, Maggie."

Her large dark eyes looked from his eyes to his hand. She returned the gesture and they shook. "You could stay. They don't expect you."

They. Darla, Kevin, Michelle. His family. His center. His balance. He shook his head, stepped back again. He looked where the loose fold of sweater drooped off her shoulder. "Your shoulder," he said.

"My best feature," she smiled.

"I can't love you."

"Control again?"

"Control," he said.

* * *

"I love you," he said, and knew it was true. Back in bed, he kissed Darla's cheek and lay back against his cool pillow. She squirmed, flopped her arm across his chest. He loved her. He could love no one else. It didn't work. It didn't fit. Unhappiness fit. Disgust. Even hatred. Divorce. They fit.

And they made room for other love, love for a woman not his wife. But he felt none of them. Wanted none of them. He did not love Maggie Dillard. Could not.

* * *

The children's squeals awakened him. As he tried to sit up, Kevin dove into bed beside him, shaking him excitedly while Michelle shook Darla. "Snow," said Kevin. "It's snowing!"

The jolt.

He swung his feet to the floor, lifted Kevin, and stumbled to the window. Outside, a thin layer of soft white snow covered the ground and piled around the few scattered toys. And more fell. Swirled near the window softening the view beyond.

"Jesus," he whispered.

"I'll get my clothes," Kevin said.

"Can we build a snowman?" Michelle said, running out of the room behind her brother.

Darla stood beside him, sleepy-eyed but smiling. She curled her arm around his waist. "It's beautiful, Aaron."

He was the first outside and stood, breathless, his face turned upward, feeling the cold flakes catch in his eyelids, melt against his cheeks. Finally, he bent, scooped a handful of snow, held it in his palm, thought of Mrs. Pipkin. And of Mrs. Delecroe. He looked toward her house, felt a wave of nausea when he saw her frail shape stretched out in the snow near her front porch. He ran toward her.

She lay flat on her back, her arms and legs outstretched as if to make a snow angel. Her pink robe and fuzzy slippers barely showed through the thin blanket of snow covering them. In death, she looked younger than he had ever seen her look in the seven years he had known her. Her wrinkles seemed smoothed away by the snow, and her mouth was frozen into a rapturous smile. An innocent smile. A child's smile. Her eyes were closed, their lashes dusted with snow.

Beside her, he saw a perfect snow angel. Perfect. No footprints indicating that its maker ever arose. No curved markings etched into the robe and wings to indicate the movement of legs and arms. Instead, the robe looked smooth, only a crease or two like a robe might really have. And the wings shaped perfectly, their tips curving up toward the head, their edges shortening as they curved in toward the body, their texture perfect, lined with feather markings. Perfect. Large and perfect. Larger than Mrs. Delecroe, even larger than he could have made. And certainly more delicate.

He knelt between Mrs. Delecroe and the snow angel, felt his jeans dampening at the knees. He studied Mrs. Delecroe's peaceful smiling face, then shifted his gaze to the perfect angel shape.

Steak Fingers

"All I want," said Katy May Stilson between gritted dentures, "is to get back into bed where I can suffer peacefully."

Samuel Stilson gripped the wheel tightly as their old Ford pickup bounced along the deeply rutted dirt road leading from their house to the highway. He chuckled. "All you want is a good meal out, and I aim to give it to you." He lifted one knobby, liver-spotted hand from the wheel and squeezed her bony shoulder. "Steak fingers, Katy May. Remember how you used to love them steak fingers every Sunday after church? Why, I remember times you'd eat two or three orders."

"I never did such." Katy adjusted her bifocals, which continually slipped on her nose, and crossed her nearly fleshless arms across her chest. This ride would kill her, she knew. It would probably shake loose one of the many blood clots those smart aleck San Antonio doctors told her she didn't have. When one of those clots reached your heart, you were as dead as a headless chicken. Katy knew that, even if the doctors didn't. Apparently none of them read *Reader's Digest*.

Samuel chuckled. "Yes sir, steak fingers, fries, and a strawberry shake. We'll get all your old favorites."

"Why don't you just put a bullet through my head, you old fool. It would be messier but just as effective." She pushed her glasses back into place and recrossed her arms. "Now will you please just get me back home and into bed."

"I'm trying to fatten you up, Katy, not kill you. A body can't just lay around in bed waiting to die." Samuel eased the truck across the cattle guard and onto the highway, then added, "That's sort of like watching the pot; it'll never boil that way."

137

"It's sinful, Samuel Stilson." Katy tilted the air conditioning vent toward her face. "It's downright sinful you dragging me out of bed into a day so hot it could singe the pinfeathers off a duck. And me having one of my worst spells in years."

"Everyone's the worst in years," Samuel chuckled.

Katy's eyes narrowed angrily behind her bifocals. He always laughed about her suffering. Or else he simply ignored her complaints. And once he had even gone so far as to say she was full, not of blood clots, but of horse droppings. He simply did not know how to grow old and sick gracefully; worse yet, he would not let her do so. Despite his eye surgery, cataracts had nearly blinded him, and the arthritis in his left leg would have put a sane man in a wheelchair. He chose, however, to ignore various doctors' advice about slowing down. But what angered Katy most was that while he ignored his own doctors he fully agreed with hers.

Katy was prone to various ailments for which no doctor could account, and Samuel seemed even less eager than the doctors to believe her. Severe leg pains sometimes kept her in bed for days at a time; intestinal suffering allowed her to consume only fresh lettuce, cottage cheese, prunes, and Baskin-Robbins ice cream; her heart murmured so loudly that it often kept her awake at night; and dizzy spells usually kept her—when the leg pains didn't—from standing in the kitchen long enough to fix a meal. Samuel remained unsympathetic. He simply did not know how to treat an old woman.

"Beachum Strother," Katy said, feeling her forehead for early signs of heat stroke. "Now he wouldn't be dragging a sick old woman out into this deadly heat."

"Beachum Strother, Beachum Strother," Samuel mimicked. "Seems like all I hear about since his brother's funeral is Beachum Strother."

"At least he knew how to treat a woman."

Samuel snorted. "How to stroke a woman's ego is what you mean. And not just *a* woman either. More like every little gal in this county." Squinting against the late morning sun, Samuel flipped the dusty visor down. He chuckled. "Stroke 'em and poke 'em, that's all Beachum Strother was ever good for. You should just be glad you wasn't one of 'em."

Katy blushed, but convinced herself it was from the heat. "What if

I was?"

"For one thing, I'd of never married you."

Katy adjusted her glasses. "I always was short on God's blessings."

"And long on Satan's hot air," Samuel smiled. She almost replied, then simply turned toward the window muttering to herself.

Katy had not seen Beachum Strother since he turned seventeen, stole his father's Studebaker pickup, and ran off to California. But when she heard from Maggie Latham, her nearest neighbor and Beachum's sister, that Beachum would be in town for their oldest brother's funeral, she considered hunting him up and running away with him. He had offered to take her that first time fifty years ago. Maybe he would still be willing. At sixty-nine, she felt far too old for such antics. Still, Beachum had once known how to treat a young lady, and she bet he knew how to treat an old lady now. Which was more than she could say for Samuel. So when Beachum came home for his oldest brother's funeral she saw her chance to be spirited away by the man who, once an extraordinary cuddler, might now be a sympathetic coddler.

But August heat always treated Katy poorly, and the day of the funeral had come and gone before she could work herself up to struggling into something other than a floppy house dress and bedroom slippers and braving the scorching Texas temperatures beyond her front door. Two days after the funeral, she had called Maggie, who reported angrily that Beachum had shown up only minutes before the service and disappeared immediately afterwards. He had apparently become, Maggie lamented, a true blue Californian, which placed him on a level with such things as sidewinders, cockroaches, and cow patties and certainly far outside anything she wished to claim as family. Sure that she had missed her one chance to be treated properly in her old age, Katy fell prey to even more ailments than usual and took to her bed for three days before Samuel almost literally dragged her from between the sheets, demanded that she put on her best dress, and coaxed her into their old Ford pickup.

On the outskirts of town, they passed the Heart O' Texas Motel and turned into the Dairy Queen parking lot next door. "Okay," Samuel said, "let's go get some meat back on those old bones." He poked her ribs and she squeezed herself closer against the door to escape his prodding fingers.

"Don't waste your wheezy old breath trying to talk me into suicide with a steak finger," she said. She poked at her glasses. "You hobble on in there if you like. But I'm sitting right here until your brain unaddles and you get me home to my bed."

Samuel frowned and rubbed his stubbled chin. Finally, he shook his head, chuckled, and said, "Suit yourself." When he stepped out of the truck, his legs buckled. He gripped the open door to steady himself. As he stood there, Katy felt sure he would soon clamber back in and take her home. Instead, he grinned at her and slammed the door.

Katy squinted through the pickup's dusty windshield and the Dairy Queen's smudged plate glass as Samuel limped up to the counter inside. He removed his white straw cowboy hat, wiped his forehead on his sleeve, and spoke to the young, stringy-haired waitress. The waitress laughed, tossing her dirty brown hair back over her shoulders.

"Damned old fool," Katy muttered. She pulled a small handkerchief with tatted edges from her purse and dabbed at her perspiring face. "Dragging me out in this heat so he can flirt with some teenage whore." To her mind, Samuel had always been a flirt, and the women who responded had always been whores. In their youth, his flirting had been all right, even cute at times, she thought. But in old age it was positively disgusting. Especially when she sat in the blistering heat aching from head to toe and waiting for him to come to his senses and take her home.

The Ford's paint appeared to bubble and melt as the August heat rippled across the hood. Realizing both windows were still up, Katy fumbled with the broken crank on her side, muttering as the window inched down. The effort exhausted her. She dabbed at her forehead with the handkerchief, then moved her hand to her thinning, wispy, gray hair. It had been pretty, once, long ago, she thought. Not stringy like the mop on that hussy inside. Samuel had said so. Beachum had said so too. Now, Samuel only chuckled and rubbed his own bald head when she complained how thin her hair was getting. Beachum would sympathize, she was sure. Beachum knew how to treat a woman.

She felt dizzy from the heat and let her head flop back against the seat. A vision of Beachum Strother wavered before her. She closed her eyes and let the vision engulf her. On the night of his seventeenth birthday, Beachum had requested an hour of Katy's time down by the lake where, he said, the stars' reflections shimmered like diamonds afire. At the lake, he had requested her clothes so that, he said, she could feel the warmth of those fiery diamonds dance across her supple white flesh. Katy could never remember whether the next request had been his or hers, but in either case Beachum took not only her clothes, but also her breath away several times before the hour she had promised him whizzed to an end. And then he had requested her company on his runaway drive to California. Although her strict Baptist upbringing had lost out to his first requests, it won against his last, and Katy went crying softly back to the bed from which she had crept an hour or so earlier, the bed in which her young husband Samuel lay snoring loudly.

Beachum had promised her the big city, bright lights, pheasant under glass, and fine wine. She had settled for the Texas hill country, steak fingers, and strawberry shakes.

Beachum Strother had definitely known how to treat a woman. And Katy did not regret that he had treated her. But neither did she regret that she had stayed behind. Not until recently, anyway. No man, including Samuel, had ever before or since made her feel what she felt that night by the lake. She had found, though, that one night sufficed. Knowing another man had wanted her—a man whose touch had vibrated every nerve in her body—satisfied her. She had lived happily with the memory of Beachum's electrifying, fleeting touch and, because of that memory, even more happily with the reality of Samuel's steady protectiveness. Until recently. That is, until old age set in and Samuel failed to protect her from its ravages or comfort her once she had been ravaged.

Katy moaned in the truck cab, wishing she had felt strong enough to get out of the house and find Beachum Strother when he arrived for his brother's funeral. He would have comforted her. She patted her forehead with her handkerchief. She tried to open her eyes, but found the lids too heavy to lift.

"Katy May Stilson," a voice whispered, and it sounded exactly as Beachum Strother's voice had sounded when he came tapping at her bedroom window fifty years before.

"Beachum Strother?" Katy said. She struggled to open her eyes. "Beachum?" With half-lifted eyelids, she peered at the figure by her door. "Beach? Is that really you?"

"So far as I know," the voice said. "Unless one of us is dreaming."

His voice sounded so young, so much like it had fifty years before, that as Katy focused her eyes she expected to see a seventeen-year-old Beachum Strother standing before her—tall and broad-shouldered, grinning that wide ingenuous grin she remembered, his green eyes sparkling with reflected starlight. What she saw, instead, was a sixty-seven-year-old Beachum Strother, still tall and broad-shouldered, the grin still ingenuous though not quite so wide, the green eyes still bright but now topped by bushy white eyebrows and underlined with wrinkles. Katy felt a surge of energy and sat straight up, her eyes wide open.

"I thought you left," she said after catching her breath.

"I did," he said and then laughed. "A very long time ago."

"No, I mean—"

"I know what you mean."

"Maggie said—"

"Maggie's a fool."

The surge left her and again she felt dizzy and limp. When she shook her head to clear it, her glasses slipped far down on her nose. "What are you doing here? How did you find me?"

"I'm here for you, Katy. I've always known where you were." He looked dim and insubstantial through her watery eyes, but when he opened the door and gripped her elbow she felt how substantial his hold was. "Can you spare an hour?" She meant to say yes, of course she could spare an hour; she had done it once without question and this second time felt no different. But overcome by his presence and, perhaps, the heat, she collapsed against him unable to speak. "I'll carry you," he said.

She felt his still-strong arms slip under her back and legs, felt him lift her effortlessly, felt her cheek rub softly against his shirt with each long smooth stride he took. "But the lake is so far," she murmured.

"I've carried your memory thousands of miles," he whispered in her ear. "I figure I can get you where you want to go now."

The sound of water lapping at the shore roused her, but when she opened her eyes all she saw was a yellowed ceiling with a gaudy light fixture. She raised her head. Beachum sat slumped in a chair near the bed, fanning himself with a TV Guide, his sweaty shirt unbuttoned. "You were right," he grinned. "Couldn't make it farther than my motel room."

"But the water," she said. "I hear water."

"It's the bathtub, Katy. For effect."

She let her head fall back and laughed, the first spontaneous laughter she had experienced for a very long time. She heard Beachum laughing, too, and the water running and the air conditioner whirring. The air felt crisp, almost cold. Her laughter brought tears to her eyes, and their sticky warmth as they trickled down her temples seemed to clear her mind, as if whatever had been fogging it were seeping out with them. "You're just the same, Beach." She sat up, still laughing. "Just as I remember." She poked at the bridge of her nose, felt no glasses there. And yet she saw him with absolute clarity, almost unnatural clarity, like the details one spots in a photograph but never notices in life. He slumped in the chair, his green eyes vibrantly alive but the rest of him obviously exhausted. "No," she said, and her laughter subsided. "You're older. You really have gotten older."

"It happens, Katy. To all of us."

"Not you, Beach. You've always been seventeen."

He dropped the TV Guide on the small round table next to him, sat up and leaned forward, elbows propped on knees. "No, Katy May. God knows how I lived past seventeen, but here I am all the way to sixty-seven." His green eyes shifted from her to the floor. "The 'Golden Years,' they say. Truth to tell, I've found little more than tarnished brass."

"You've found more than I."

"No, Katy." Suddenly out of the chair and beside her on the bed, he held her hand. "You've got the gold."

"Look at me," she scoffed. "I'm sick and scrawny and weak. But you, you're still strong and tall and healthy."

He shrugged. "Maybe some," he said and then, grinning, "I can still manage a roll in the clover. Well, sometimes I can."

"See," she said, grinning with him.

"But mostly I have no one to roll with."

"You never married, did you? Everybody said you wouldn't." She shivered in the cold, vaguely wondering how she could speak with him so calmly after waiting so long to see him.

"Sure I did. Even got so I liked it the sixth time."

"Sixth time!"

"Yeah. She was a beauty, too. Smooth, supple, white flesh, just like yours used to be. But when she realized nothing she could do would unwrinkle mine, she headed for less furrowed fields." Katy felt the tears again, only this time they seemed to muddy her thoughts rather than clear them. Beachum kissed her lightly on the cheek, then held her at arm's length and laughed. "Kissing with dentures is hell, isn't it?"

She tried to smile. "I don't know."

"You mean you still have your original chompers?"

"No. I mean I don't . . . we haven't—"

"You and Sammy boy don't kiss! Why, Katy May Stilson, you're the last person I thought would be taken in by that old-age propaganda. We may not have what the young folks have and what we've got may not always work quite right, but we can by God still use it." He pulled her to him, removed the glasses she had thought were missing, and kissed her fully on the mouth, holding her there until his upper lip suddenly caved in. He leaned back, shoved his upper teeth back into place with his thumb. "See what I mean?" She giggled and nodded. "It's hell with dentures. But even worse without them—you can't get any suction with an inside-out pucker."

Katy giggled still more—truly giggled, she realized, as if she were a girl again. She did not notice that he had jumped up, but she saw him as a blur when he pulled the curtains closed, bounded to the light switch, clicked it off, and leapt back into bed. "Look," he said, producing a tiny flashlight on a keyring shaped like California. Pointing it toward the ceiling, he flicked the light on and off rapidly, again and again. "Almost like stars," he said, "like diamonds afire."

"Almost," she laughed and folded her thin arms around him. He pitched the flashlight to the floor and returned her gesture. She squeezed her eyes shut, listened to the running water, felt his strong embrace, waited for the vibration in her nerves. Try as she might, she did not feel it.

144

She felt happy and warm and strong, but not electrified. "Almost," she said again. "But not quite."

"Never quite," he whispered. "But it's all we've got, and that's okay." When she opened her eyes, the gaudy light fixture was back on and brilliant sunlight shone through the window, its curtains wide open. She had never felt him leave her side, and he still hugged her tightly. "Come with me," he said.

She smiled sadly. "The hour's up, isn't it?"

"Yes," he said, "and then some."

"I've lived only an hour in fifty years, Beach."

"No, Katy. You've lived fifty years in an hour."

He lifted her into his arms, and the next thing she felt was a furnace blast of hot air as he stepped outside. Her skin prickled and she immediately began perspiring. But rather than weakening her, the heat seemed to burn away the pains she feared would return. She felt her heart beating hard and steadily, pumping clean blood through her unclogged veins. Her stomach growled. "I can walk," she said. "I'll walk from here." He set her down, and when she turned to say goodbye, he already sat in his truck, the same Studebaker he had stolen from his father fifty years before. It started noiselessly. As he turned it toward the highway, he looked back and winked, his green eyes flashing in the sunlight.

"Katy May, Katy May!" Turning away from the highway and back toward the Dairy Queen, she saw Samuel, his bald head glinting in the sun, hobbling toward her as quickly as he could. Behind him, several people scurried around the parking lot, peering into cars, between cars, and even under cars.

One of them ran up beside Samuel, then yelled back at the others, "He found her!" Katy squinted toward them and recognized her as the waitress with stringy hair. She pushed her bifocals up on her nose, breathed deeply, and walked briskly to meet them.

Samuel hugged her tightly. "You damned old crazy woman, where've you been?"

"Don't be angry," she said, hugging him back. "I've been with Beachum Strother."

Samuel released her, his brows arched. "Beachum Strother!"

"Beachum Strother!" the stringy-haired girl echoed. "Ain't he Maggie Latham's brother. The one that didn't die, I mean."

"That's the one," Katy said.

The girl pulled thoughtfully on a strand of her unwashed hair. "But Miz Latham was in for coffee the other day after the funeral, and she was cussin' his name somethin' awful because he took off right after. Didn't even talk to nobody."

"Maggie's a fool," Katy smiled.

Samuel and the girl exchanged quizzical glances, but when the girl began to speak, he raised a finger to his lips. He put his arm gently around Katy's shoulder and began guiding her back toward their old Ford. "It's all right, Katy," he said. He was not chuckling. "You just need a little rest. I never should of brung you out in this heat. I'll make it up to you, though, I promise. Anything you want, I'll—"

"Stop babbling, you old fool," Katy said. When Samuel's arm slipped from her shoulder, she realized her step was too quick for his arthritic leg. She paused for him to catch up. "All I want," she said, gripping his elbow to help him along, "is to go home to bed." He opened the truck door for her, and when she had settled into the seat she turned to look directly into his dark brown eyes. "With you," she said. About to shut the door, Samuel instead clutched it to keep from falling. Blushing, the young waitress helped steady him, then quickly entered the Dairy Queen. Samuel stared wide-eyed at Katy, his mouth open. "Don't worry," she said, patting his knobby hand, "I won't ask for anything you can't give."

Samuel's jaw moved up and down, but no words came out. Finally, he stammered, "But—what—will—we—do?"

She shrugged, then chuckled. "We'll open the curtains wide, cuddle up, and watch for the stars to come out. Then . . . well, then we'll see."

Samuel shook his head, blinked, whispered, "Godamighty." He slammed the door, then poked his head through the open window. "Don't go away, Katy. Don't go anywhere. I just have to get my hat."

As he limped quickly toward the Dairy Queen door, Katy's stomach growled again. "Samuel," she called. He paused in the doorway to look back. "Get some steak fingers, too."

"Godamighty!" he yelled. She chuckled.

Salvation

What if a man said, "Hey, God—" and what if he really meant it, meant it with all his heart and soul, with every inch of his being—what if he said, "Hey, God, I'll do anything—*anything*—if you'll just send me a woman"? This is what Charlie Don Atwood wondered, and Charlie Don Atwood wanted a woman. He was not smart, he was not good looking, and he was not rich. But he wanted a woman. And so he wondered about asking God.

"What if?" he said to Cecil Voss one day as they stood drinking Cokes and waiting for customers at Cecil's Gulf station. He poured a package of salted peanuts down the neck of his Coke bottle. "What do you think?" His deep, resonant voice sounded as if it might vibrate the ribs of anyone listening.

Cecil, short and fat with a wad of snuff perpetually bulging in his lower lip, chuckled and sat down behind his desk. "You go take care of her," he said, nodding toward the blue Ford Fairmont that had just pulled up. "I'll be thinking about it."

After pumping the gas, Charlie Don was just handing the woman her credit card and thanking her when she looked up at him and said, "Praise God."

He stood for a moment wondering what to answer. She smiled at him, her acne scars crinkling. "Right," he said.

"Imogene Bates," she said, extending a tiny pale hand through her open window.

"Charlie Don Atwood." He shook her hand briefly, careful not to squeeze too hard.

She squinted at him from behind thick-lensed glasses with large gray frames. "You're new, aren't you?"

"Couple months."

"I don't drive much."

Charlie Don nodded, smiled. "If you don't mind my askin', do you know a lot about God?"

"My father," she said, "he's a preacher."

"I've been wonderin'. If I asked, do you suppose God would send a woman my way?"

Her acne scars uncrinkled. "You pig," she said between clenched teeth. He leaned against the unleaded pump and watched her drive away, squinting against the sun's blinding reflection on the Fairmont's bumper.

Cecil was laughing when Charlie Don stepped back inside. "Now you know why I sent you out there," he said.

Charlie Don reached for his Coke on Cecil's desk. "You know her?"

"She stops in every now and then."

"She told me to praise God."

"When you're as ugly as her you gotta believe real hard in God. Otherwise you got nobody to blame it on." Cecil laughed.

"I asked her would God mind me askin' for a woman," said Charlie Don, not laughing. He swigged his Coke, chewed the peanuts that came with it.

"Say," said Cecil, winking at Charlie Don, "word is she's desperate."

"She called me a pig." Charlie Don's deep voice sounded puzzled but calm.

"She was probably lookin' in her rear-view," Cecil chuckled.

Charlie Don smoothed his mustache with thumb and forefinger, rubbed his beard with his palm. "She said her daddy's a preacher."

"I've heard."

"I'm thinkin' maybe he could help me."

"Sure," Cecil said, smirking and thumbing the day's receipts. "Word is he's next to God himself. Him and his ugly daughter and his Choir of Praise over to the Holy Church of the Blood of the Lord Jesus."

Charlie Don finished his Coke, slid the empty into the wire rack by the machine. "Where's that?"

* * *

The Holy Church of the Blood of the Lord Jesus was small, but it had a very high ceiling and was empty, so Reverend Garvin Bates's words echoed into distortion before Charlie Don could make them out. The reverend, too, was distorted. The church dark but for a single bright floor lamp behind the pulpit where he stood, he seemed only a swaying, indistinct shadow outlined by brilliant light. Charlie Don walked toward him. The echoing voice stopped in mid-sentence.

"I'm busy with the Lord's work," the shadow said. "Practicing for Sunday." Then he leaned on the pulpit and sighed. "A preacher's work is never done."

Charlie Don shoved his hands into his jeans pockets. "I was just wonderin' about God." His voice seemed to fill the tiny church all the way to its high exposed beams.

"Praise the Lord!" the reverend shouted, his high voice a striking contrast to Charlie Don's deep one. He lifted his hands toward the ceiling and raised his shadowy face toward them as if examining his fingernails. "That voice. That voice!" he shouted. Charlie Don hadn't heard the voice, but he, too, looked up, mainly to avoid looking at the stained-glass image of Jesus that served as a window behind the pulpit. Jesus hung on the cross, his cheeks hollow, his eyes sunken, blood dripping into them from his forehead, blood dripping from his hands, blood dripping from his side, blood dripping from his feet. Above his head, an inscription read, *His blood flowed freely*, and beneath the cross it continued, *That our spirits might be cleansed.*

Charlie Don flinched when the reverend suddenly slapped his palms against the pulpit. "Sing for me," he yelled at Charlie Don.

"What?"

"Sing for me. Sing for God. Sing your guts out, boy!" He slapped the pulpit again, but then stood very erect, calmly folded his arms across his chest, and quietly said, "'O come, let us sing unto the Lord: let us make a joyful noise to the rock of our salvation.'"

Charlie Don shook his head, stepped backwards. "My singin' ain't too joyful."

The arms unfolded with an audible snap at the elbows and a hand with a pointing finger shot out toward Charlie Don. "You must sing. That voice. That perfect bass voice! Do you not understand?"

Charlie Don shifted his weight. "Not much."

"The Lord God Almighty sent you here, son. Sent you for you and your salvation and for me and my choir." He straightened, laughed, clasped his hands together. "Best darned choir this side of heaven. The envy of every preacher in town."

Charlie Don scratched his beard. "I'm not much on church. Don't know no hymns. What it is, I was just wonderin' would God mind me askin' for somethin'."

"Mind? Mind! Listen, boy: 'Ask, and ye shall receive, that your joy may be full.'" Charlie Don grinned when the reverend paused. "But," Reverend Bates grinned back, "'Unto whomsoever much is given, of him shall much be required.'"

Charlie Don shoved his hands in his pockets, squinted at the shadowy figure before him. "I figured there'd be a catch."

"May the good Lord God forgive you, boy." The reverend leaned on the pulpit, raised his voice slightly. "Do you not want to praise God?" Charlie Don shrugged. The reverend raised his voice even more. "Do you not want to give unto the Lord?" Another shrug. The reverend stamped his foot, shouted, "Do you not want your prayers answered?" His high voice echoed into the back of the church.

"Sure," said Charlie Don. "Yeah."

"Then you must sing," and he pounded on the pulpit with each word.

Charlie Don shrugged. "I don't know. I ain't never sang much. I guess I could try."

The reverend stood erect, folded his arms, spoke in the deepest, calmest voice he had yet used. "Approach, son. Approach and pray with me. For here on earth I am God's voice, and through me you shall find the salvation you seek."

"Salvation?"

"Salvation. Redemption. Eternal spiritual bliss. God's holy presence that bathes our souls in eternal heavenly light!"

Charlie Don squinted against the shaft of light the floor lamp shot into his face when the reverend leaned aside. He said, "I was just wantin' a woman."

The reverend made a squeak in his throat. "A woman? A woman! Are you mad?" He slapped the pulpit, stamped his feet. "Our good Lord God Almighty has nothing to do with women!"

Charlie Don shook his head. "I figured," he said and walked up the aisle.

"Unless—" The reverend paused until Charlie Don stopped and turned. "Unless, of course, you mean a spiritual companion. An honest, God-fearing woman looked upon with favor in the Lord's eyes. Now that might be arranged. Beauty is but vain, son, but 'a woman that feareth the Lord, she shall be praised.'"

Charlie Don looked at the shadowed reverend, looked at the floor, shrugged. "Okay," he said. "I ain't all that picky."

* * *

He would call a special choir practice for eight that night, the reverend said, but Charlie Don should arrive early to meet everyone before they began. Charlie Don agreed. If all God wanted him to do in return for a woman was sing a little, he was willing to fulfill his end of the bargain. And maybe, he thought, God really would send him a woman.

He arrived early as instructed, but no one else was there. The church was darker than before, and he felt relieved to see that the stained glass image of Jesus was indiscernible at night. He felt his way to a pew, helped only by the dim red glow of moonlight filtering through the dark red stained-glass windows along the walls. The air conditioner running, the pews padded, he felt comfortable. He felt good. For the first time in his life he consciously thought there might really be a God. A good God who understood what a man like him wanted, needed. He closed his eyes and tried to imagine the kind of woman such a God would send him.

"It's nice in here," a voice said, and he knew it was Imogene Bates. "Don't you think so?" She slid into the pew.

He shrugged. "Yeah." He squinted to see her in the dim red light, her pock-marked face, her crooked nose, the pull in her upper lip that exposed her front teeth even with her mouth closed.

"Imogene Bates," she said. "Remember?"

"Sure. Charlie Don Atwood."

"You're staring."

"It's dark."

Silent, she stared back. Then she looked away. "I'm not pretty."

"It ain't all that dark."

"You're a cruel man."

"You called me a pig."

"I'm sorry I called you a pig."

He shrugged again. "I'm sorry you're ugly."

"Then again, perhaps you are a pig."

"I didn't mean nothin'. I mean, I'm no prize myself."

"Well," she said, then paused. She looked at the hymnal in her lap, traced an imaginary line around its cover with her finger. "Perhaps you could be."

He waited, but she said no more. "Yeah?"

"Physical beauty, Mr. Atwood, is but vain."

"I've heard that."

"Did you mean it, what you told my father?"

"I don't mind singin' a little, I guess."

"That's not what I meant." She shook her head. "Never mind. But listen—" She looked at him, her eyes intense, the red glow of filtered moonlight reflecting off her glasses. "It's not just the singing. It's the praise in your heart that leads to understanding, to knowing, to revelation." She reached for his arm, seemed desperate to grab him, but apparently thought better of it and withdrew her hand. "To redemption, Mr. Atwood. To salvation. To God's holy light." She breathed quickly, almost gasping. "You want that, don't you?" He shrugged. She said, "I want you," and then violently shaking her head, "No, I mean I want that for you."

"Mostly," he said, "I just want a woman."

Her shoulders slumped. "I know." She reached for him again, again pulled back, this time gripping her hymnal tightly with both hands.

"Are you educated?"

"Some. Ninth grade."

"Never mind. I think you could be a good man. Are you a good man? You seem like you could be a good man."

Charlie Don scratched his beard, considered her words, both what she said and what she seemed to mean. Maybe she was the one. "We're early," he finally said.

"Yes."

"I was thinkin'," he said, squinting at the profile of her downcast face. "You want to go to my place or somethin'?"

She suddenly sat very erect, glared at him. "Mr. Atwood, neither the Lord nor I approve of wanton sex."

He sighed, nodded. "That's okay. I wasn't wantin' it that bad."

"Wanton, Mr. Atwood. *Wanton*. The meaningless, flagrant abuse of the body our Lord has lent us." She leaned close, her breath minty-sweet with mouthwash. "The body is nothing, Mr. Atwood. It is dust and shall return to dust. Jesus Christ knew: he gave up his body, let his blood flow freely so our spirits could be redeemed. The soul, the soul our dear Lord has given us is everything. It is pure and it is light. Pure light. White light. But the man who abuses the body is lower than the dirt from which it came, and his soul must be purged by the fires of hell!"

She trembled, and he wanted to grasp her shoulders to steady her. "Is it me that's got to be purged?"

She clutched his arm, released it, clutched again. "It doesn't have to be." The strength of her tiny hands amazed him. He would never have guessed that those pale hands, which he could have believed were more soul than body, could cling so tightly, could squeeze so deeply into his flesh. As he looked where she clung to him, she looked too. She gasped, jerked her hands away, clung to her hymnal. "My dear man," she said quietly, "it does not have to be. Let me save you."

He smoothed his mustache, cocked his head to look at her. "Okay," he said.

* * *

155

He was surprised. He actually enjoyed the singing. When he sang, when they all sang together, he felt good, and he felt as if they all felt good. Then, as a gesture, he would reach over and squeeze Imogene's tiny pale hand in his large one. She would momentarily squeeze back, but then, looking down at their entwined hands, she would scowl and pull away.

"You have a natural talent," she said as they walked into the parking lot after their third evening of practice. He shoved his hands in his pockets, smiled. She stopped by her car, the single parking lot light shining on her, reflecting off the thick lenses of her glasses. She smiled at a couple who sang in the choir, waited for them to pass, then said, "When you sing, do you feel anything special?"

He looked at the ground, pulled on his beard. *I don't mind that you're ugly*, he might have said. *When we're singin', it don't matter*. But that would probably be the wrong thing to say. "No," he said.

Her smile faded. "Well, never mind. Just remember," she said as she started to turn away, "remember that your voice is a gift from God, and in singing you are thanking him for it." She looked up into his face, began smiling again. "Remember that, Mr. Atwood, and it will happen. Suddenly one night you will feel giddy, lighter than air, dizzy; and everything you look at will be bathed in beautiful light, white light, pure light." She trembled, as she always did when she spoke of God, Jesus, and salvation. She clasped her hands at her chest, gazed skyward. "Then you will know that God has touched your soul. Then you will know that you have found salvation!"

"Okay," Charlie Don said, and then, hesitantly, "Is that when I'll get me a woman?"

"Oh, Mr. Atwood!" She stamped her foot, stared at him, her mouth closed, her face reddening. Suddenly her tiny hands shot out and clenched his forearms, and again he was surprised at the strength of her grip. "I'm the . . . If you only . . . If I could . . . ." Her entire face wrinkled as she squeezed her eyes shut and shook her head as if trying to rattle the words into place. But when she opened her eyes, she seemed shocked to find him there, gasped, released his arms, and scrambled into her Fairmont.

He watched the red glow of her tail lights until they disappeared around the corner by the Safeway three blocks away. He frowned, shook his head, removed his denim jacket as he ambled to his truck.

* * *

As usual, he couldn't sleep, so, as usual, he sat outside his small trailer on the edge of town drinking beer and wondering if he should stop fooling himself about God and women. When it began to rain, he stepped inside and flicked on the television. Just as he stretched out on his battered couch, someone knocked insistently on his front door.

"Hi," a young woman said when he opened the door. She stepped inside and extended her hand to him. "I'm Deanne Baccus." She shook hands only briefly but squeezed hard. Although wet, her hand felt warm. She giggled and ran her fingers through her wet hair. "Don't ask, I already know the questions. I never talk about where I'm from, I don't know where I'm going—California, maybe—I'm nineteen, I hitch hike everywhere I go and bum whatever food and money I can, and I need a dry place to sleep tonight." He watched her hair shimmer in the glow of his overhead light. "So, if you're cool with that, I'd be obliged. If not," and she finished with a shrug.

"Okay," he said and closed the door.

* * *

Showered and dried, she sat on the edge of his bed wearing one of his work shirts with an orange globe that said GULF across the pocket. It reached almost to her ankles, but she crossed her legs so that the tail fell open to her knees, where the bottom button held it closed.

"Really," she said, "the couch will be fine."

Standing in the doorway, he shook his head. "I'm gonna watch some TV anyway."

"Thanks. You're nice."

He pulled at his mustache, started to speak, paused, finally said, "I asked God for a woman."

She giggled. "You're kidding."

He shrugged. "Good night."

"Hey." He had almost reached the living room when she called. "I'm not a virgin."

He looked back. Backlighted by the bedside lamp, her hair shown brightly around her shadowed face. "Me neither," he said.

She stopped combing her hair, looked at him steadily. "What I mean is, you've been real nice. I'd be happy to, you know, pay."

He rubbed his beard. "You believe in God?"

"Not much."

"A friend of mine, she believes real hard. Me, I ain't sure."

"Look, God didn't send me here. But . . . you know . . . if you want a woman . . . ."

"I don't know. I mean you comin' along just when you did, out of nowhere, and just happenin' to stop here."

She shrugged. "It happened."

"My friend, she says God works in mysterious ways."

"I guess," she said. "I've got a cousin who was born with no arms." He raised his eyebrows but said nothing. She started at her hair again. "So anyway, about my offer, just let me know."

It would be easy, he thought. But if she weren't the one, accepting her offer might ruin his chances of ever getting the right one. He nodded slowly. "Yeah. I'll let you know."

* * *

The next day, Sunday, held two surprises for Charlie Don. First, he felt compelled to remain alert throughout Reverend Garvin Bates's entire sermon, the time he usually spent slipping in and out of daydreams about what kind of woman God would send him. "'The lips of a strange woman drop as honeycomb,'" the reverend began, glaring down from the pulpit straight at Charlie Don, "'and her mouth is smoother than oil: But her end is bitter as wormwood, sharp as a two-edged sword.'"

As usual, Reverend Bates clapped and stamped and pointed and shouted about the sins of the flesh and the bright holy spot of the soul. But this time, something in the words kept pulling at Charlie Don's attention. And the reverend seemed to speak to him alone. "'As a jewel of gold in a swine's snout, so is a fair woman which is without discretion.'" Charlie Don squirmed in his pew.

158

The second surprise was Imogene. During the final hymn when he had, for the moment, forgotten the sermon, when he felt good and felt that everyone else felt good, Imogene clutched his hand and didn't let go. She squeezed until the last note faded into silence.

"Go peacefully, brothers and sisters," the reverend said, and still she held his hand, pressing it down on the pew so her father would not see. "'Let us walk honestly in the day; not in rioting and drunkenness, not in chambering and wantonness, not in strife and envy. But put ye on the Lord Jesus Christ, and make no provisions for the flesh, to fulfill the lusts thereof.'" He stepped down from the pulpit and walked, hands folded, head bowed, toward the door, the people in each pew filing out after him as he passed.

Imogene released Charlie Don's hand as her father passed their pew, but she did not join the recessional. Her glance indicated that Charlie Don should wait with her. When the church had emptied, her father outside visiting with parishioners, Imogene reached for Charlie Don's hand again, but changed her mind and looked away from him instead.

"A woman stayed with you last night."

His eyes widened. "How'd you know?"

"Never mind."

He pulled at his mustache, studied the pattern of light, red from filtering through the stained-glass windows, on her hair.

"She wants to stay awhile."

She finally looked at him, her eyes drooping behind her thick lenses. "And you're going to let her?"

"She's wore out. Hitch hikes everywhere." He squeezed her shoulder; she let him. "Imogene, it ain't because you're ugly."

She looked down, fidgeted with the sash of her red and white pin-striped dress. "That always comes up, doesn't it?"

"But really. Every time we sing, I feel good, and I look at you and think, 'It ain't that she's ugly.' It's just—I don't know—there's somethin' ain't there. It ain't your fault."

"It is my fault."

"No. It ain't your fault." He glanced toward the back of the church to be sure the door was closed, the reverend still outside. Then he leaned

159

toward her and meant to kiss her cheek, but she suddenly clutched the nape of his neck with both hands and kissed him fully on the lips. Surprised by the quickness of her action, his automatic reaction was to pull back, but she clung so tightly that he couldn't. Then, just as suddenly as she had grabbed him, she let go, gasped, stared at him wide-eyed. His lips burned. He touched where the bottom one had split from the force she had exerted, looked at the blood on his fingers.

"Oh," she gasped.

"It's okay."

"Oh my." She cowered in the pew, her hands held out as if to repel him, even though he no longer leaned close.

"Really, it's okay. I'll put some ice on it."

"Oh my God!" She stumbled out of the pew and ran for the door.

* * *

Charlie Don didn't go to work that afternoon, nor did he go home where Deanne said she'd probably be sleeping most of the day. He drove around town until one o'clock, when the convenience stores began selling beer. He loaded an ice chest with Lone Star and spent the rest of the day drinking and driving the winding back roads of the county.

At night, he ate in town at a honky-tonk joint where the only light was a hazy purple glow created by red and blue beer signs lining the walls of a huge smoke-filled room that served as diner, pool hall, and dance hall. He drank cold beer from icy mugs, shot pool with back-slapping strangers, and danced with a waitress named Ardyth during her breaks. As they danced, he sang along quietly with the not-so-good local band. Ardyth said he sang better than they did, and he believed her. He was grateful to Reverend Garvin Bates and his daughter Imogene for getting him to sing. He liked it. It felt good. Better here, though, than in church, and best of all as he danced with a waitress named Ardyth who said he sang well and who never said a word about God, Jesus, or salvation.

This was the place for him, these the songs for him. Mostly slow songs, and mostly sad, but all of them about people, about making love, fighting, drinking, divorcing, and making love again. Real songs. Flesh and blood songs.

Somewhere between the time Ardyth told him he'd better sit down and the time she woke him at closing time, it occurred to him how important Jesus really had been, if what they said about Him was true. More important than Reverend Garvin Bates knew. More important than his ugly daughter Imogene could ever understand. He thought of the stained-glass image of Jesus, the sunken eyes, the hollow cheeks, the sadness. Flesh and blood, that's what it was all about. Forget what He might or might not have accomplished for the spirit, right or wrong Jesus had given up the only sure thing. And Charlie Don was betting that He hadn't done it as freely as the folks at the Holy Church of the Blood of the Lord Jesus claimed.

"This gal I know," he said as Ardyth led him to the door, "she don't understand Jesus."

"I know, honey. Imogene Bates."

He pulled his shoulders up straight, stopped to squint at her. "You know her?"

"Sweetheart," she said, laughing and slapping his shoulder, "you've been talking about her all night."

"Yeah?" He stood staring at Ardyth, and she urged him toward the door. "Did I show you this busted lip she gave me? You know what I think?"

"You think she thought you were Jesus."

"I think she thought I was Jesus come to save her soul." He flung his arm around Ardyth and laughed.

"I know," she said. "We're closing now. Drive careful." She opened the door for him.

He kept laughing. "I mean, what with my beard and all, you know?"

"I tell you what I think." Ardyth patted his shoulder as he stumbled out the door. "I think that busted lip came from something a lot more serious than a spiritual kiss."

"Yeah?" he said, but she had already closed the door. He stood trying to remember where his truck was and thinking how quiet the night suddenly seemed. Behind the doors, the bar was silent. The parking lot was empty but for his truck, which he hadn't yet spotted off in a corner out of the light. He tried to remember the faces of the pool players, the sound of Ardyth's voice. He looked up at the stars. He felt cold.

* * *

Deanne was asleep when he got home, but she was up before him the next morning and had coffee brewed when he rolled off the couch and stumbled to the bathroom groaning about his aching head. She giggled at him when he stumbled back to the table, slumped in a chair, and used both hands to clutch the coffee cup she slid across to him.

"Bad night?" she said.

"I've been thinkin'." He slurped his coffee. "You ain't no godsend."

"I tried to tell you that," she said, and then, smiling coyly, "But I could show you a little bit of heaven."

"I know. But how come?"

She shrugged. "I needed a place. You want a woman." She got up to pour more coffee. "Anyway, I like your voice," she giggled. "It kind of vibrates my insides, you know?"

He smiled. "I like your hair. You've got pretty hair."

"Voices and hair. That's all there is really, isn't it?"

"Imogene says the soul is everything."

"Maybe. But you can't hear it. And you can't see it or touch it."

"Yeah." He scratched his beard. "You gonna be here awhile?"

"I got nowhere to go."

"Okay," he said. "I'll be back in a while."

* * *

Reverend Garvin Bates answered the door in a gold bathrobe that looked like satin, the hem of which brushed the floor. "I've been thinkin'," said Charlie Don.

"Good Lord, man," the reverend said, clutching his bathrobe as if it weren't already tied tightly around him. "It's too early."

"But I've been thinkin'. I can't sing no more."

162

The reverend's eyebrows arched, wrinkling even more the pa waxy wrinkles of his forehead. "Of course you can. You have a wonderf voice."

"I can," said Charlie Don, shoving his hands into his pockets an staring down at his boots. "But I ain't goin' to. It just don't seem right."

"Right? Right!" The reverend shoved his finger practically int Charlie Don's face. "It is imperative! You promised. You made a covenan with me, with the Lord. 'Better is it that thou shouldest not vow, than tha thou shouldest vow and not pay.'"

"What it is, I found me a woman on my own. I figure I ain' obligated no more."

"A woman!" Reverend Bates shouted, his voice a high pitched squeak. "I can guess what kind of woman you've found. The devil's woman, the devil's work. Be not tempted, Charlie Don Atwood. 'Lust not after her beauty in thine heart; neither let her take thee with her eyelids.'"

Charlie Don shook his head. "It ain't them things. It's her hair, mostly." The reverend clenched his fists, ground his teeth, puffed out his cheeks, seemed unable to speak. "I'd like to tell Imogene," Charlie Don said.

The reverend's hands shot out, the fists unclenching, as if he were reaching for Charlie Don's throat. "Absolutely not! 'Get thee behind me, Satan!'" He slammed the door, but as Charlie Don shook his head and turned to leave, the door swung open and Imogene screamed, leanin toward him in her bathrobe, her arm caught in her father's grasp.

"You can't," she said, and she was crying. "Please!"

He shoved his hands back into his pockets. "I'm sorry, Imoger It ain't your fault."

"It is," she cried. "It is my fault. Wait for me," she hollered as l father slammed the door, and then, from behind the door, "Please wa

He waited, wanting to talk with her, wanting to explain. He st listening to the muffled argument behind the door. But finally he cle heard the reverend's shrill yell: "You'll not follow him or you're no c of mine, no child of God!" Charlie Don shook his head and walked t truck.

* * *

He wanted to shower first, he told Deanne, and she said she'd be waiting. He scrubbed himself hard, twice, all over. When he finished, he dried slowly and didn't bother to dress. He studied his face in the mirror, prepared the best smile he could, and stepped out facing the bedroom.

Deanne stood naked by the bed, but she fumbled with her underwear, trying to get them back on. She had drawn the curtains so that the room was dim but for the bedside lamp behind her. As on the first night she had sat there, her hair shone with the light, but her face and figure remained shadowed. Her underwear pulled up around her knees, she paused to point down the short dark hallway. "She's crazy."

Charlie Don turned to see Imogene standing by his tiny kitchen table, her hair still tousled from overnight, her glasses off so that she squinted terribly, her white terrycloth bathrobe and red cotton nightgown crumpled around her ankles. She shivered, or trembled, he didn't know which.

"Imogene?"

"Charlie Don." Sunlight shone around her through the kitchen window. Her small pale body seemed to glow pure white.

Astounded, he stepped backwards, stepped forward, stumbled, fell to his knees. "Imogene. You?"

She pulled her shoulders back, tried to control her trembling. "I am your gift, Charlie Don, and you are mine."

He gaped at her smooth white skin her shoulders, her breasts, her belly, her thighs. "I feel it Imogene."

"Y'all are crazy as hell," said Deanne. Fully dressed, she brushed past Charlie Don, stepped around Imogene, and hurried out the door.

Imogene held her hands out, palms up, toward Charlie Don. "'Every good gift and every perfect gift is from above, and cometh from the father of lights.'"

"I see it," he said. "Like you said. I see the light. I see the white light." He tried to rise, felt himself floating up and up and up but knew he hadn't moved. He, too, stretched out his hands.

She moved toward him, her white flesh glowing brighter. "You are

164

my strength and my song, Charlie Don Atwood, and you have become my salvation." She touched his hands. She gasped, not as if frightened, but as if thrilled. "I feel giddy, Charlie Don. I feel dizzy." He clutched her hands to steady her. "Take me," she said. "Save me."

"Okay," he said and folded his massive arms around her small pale body.